Maud Flies Solo

MAUD

FLIES SOLO

by Gibbs Davis

Bradbury Press   Scarsdale, N.Y.

Library of Congress Cataloging in Publication Data
Davis, Gibbs. Maud flies solo.
Summary: Maud seeks ways to combat her loneliness when her older sister becomes interested in things that don't include a sixth-grader.
    [1. Brothers and sisters—Fiction] I. Title.
PZ7.D2886Mau   [Fic]   80-27084
ISBN 0-87888-173-5

For my mother,
Margarett Kable Russell Davis,
who nurtured the fantastical
in her youngest daughter,
with love

1

Why Is Lily Acting So Weird?

Maud didn't understand why Lily wanted to go directly to the lingerie department. She had hoped her sister would want to go to the candy section of Groman's Department Store where they were having a sale on chocolate-covered peanuts, or even down to the basement to watch a little TV. The salesman in Major Appliances always kept all three shelves of TV sets operating at the same time.

It was too late now. Lily was already in the fitting room. Maud plopped down on the rose-colored carpet and leaned back against a table overflowing with girdles. She pulled a dog-eared paperback book out of her jacket pocket, turned to a page marked with smudges and went over the checklist one more time—

TAKE-OFF (Cessna 152)
1. Wing Flaps—Up
2. Carburetor Heat—Cold
3. Throttle—Full Open
4. Elevator Control—Lift Nose Wheel at 50 mph

"Can I help you?"

Maud looked up into the tired face of a large saleswoman. She wondered whether a simple "no" would be enough of an answer or whether "not now" would be more appropriate.

"No. Not now, thank you," she said diplomatically. She looked down at her book and read the remainder of the checklist, mouthing the words carefully as she read them—

LANDING (Cessna 152)
1. Touchdown—Main Wheels First
2. Landing Roll—Lower Nose Wheel Gently
3. Braking—As Required

"I'm afraid you'll have to move," came the voice again. Maud looked up into the annoyed face. "The girdles on this table are all on sale. You're blocking traffic." Maud looked around. She didn't see anyone except two mannequins.

"You're blocking traffic," the saleswoman repeated in a stern voice, as though she were a police officer patrolling the area.

"I'm waiting for my sister," Maud said as she quickly stuffed the book into her jacket pocket and stood up. "She's in one of the fitting rooms. I think she's trying on nightgowns. Will you tell her to hurry up, please?"

"I have only one customer in the fitting rooms now and she's trying on undergarments."

That can't be Lily, Maud thought. Their mother

always took care of buying their underwear for them.

"Maybe you didn't notice her when she walked in," Maud said. "She's kind of pale. Sometimes she blends in."

The saleswoman turned around and walked into the hall of fitting rooms just as Maud was going to warn her not to tell Lily what she had said. Lily was sensitive about her pale freckled skin and white blonde hair.

Maud looked at her watch. She had been waiting for Lily to come out of the fitting room for exactly thirteen minutes. Thirteen meant two things to Maud—an unlucky number and her sister's age. She held her breath and counted seconds until the unlucky minute passed. If numbers were animals, she was certain thirteen would be a snake hiding in the grass. It wasn't anything like eleven, her own age. Since Lily turned thirteen this past summer, nothing had been the same.

Maud first noticed the mysterious and disturbing change in her older sister on the night Lily returned from camp and moved all of her things out of their room. For as long as Maud could remember, she and Lily had shared that room. It had been a mutually satisfying arrangement for several years. Maud slept on the top bunk because she liked to be in high places and Lily slept on the bottom bunk because she didn't like to be in high places. Everything was fine until Lily complained that she needed privacy and that no one her age shared a bunk bed anymore.

She slept on the sofa in the den downstairs until their mother bought a new bed and flowered curtains and helped Lily transform the den into her new bedroom.

Her mother explained that it was normal for a girl Lily's age to want a room of her own, but Maud didn't see it that way: Lily must have moved out of their room because of something she had done to make her angry. Maud had been wondering for four months now what it was she had done.

Maud picked up one of the girdles lying on the table next to her and stretched it as far as it would go. Suddenly, as though with a will of its own, the elastic pants snapped from her fingers and soared halfway across the room. Maud looked around to see if anyone had noticed the flying undergarment.

The girdle had landed beneath a rack of nightgowns. Maud quickly returned it to the table and walked back to the nightgowns. She looked at each one carefully, trying to imagine whether Lily would like it. Months ago, Lily had promised that they would get matching nightgowns, but every time Maud wanted to go shopping for them Lily was doing something with her new friend, Claire. If Claire hadn't been busy babysitting, Maud never would have had the chance to go shopping with Lily after school today.

Claire was the kind of girl who wore bright red nail polish. As far as Maud was concerned, that was all that needed to be said.

She was beginning to suspect that Lily might have

wanted to come to the lingerie department to secretly buy their matching nightgowns. She's not letting me know about it because she wants it to be a surprise, Maud thought. She imagined Lily sneaking upstairs during dinner tonight to lay one of the matching nightgowns on her bed. Any minute now Lily would walk slowly out of the fitting rooms with a smile on her face, carrying a large bag with the top rolled over so Maud couldn't see what was inside. Only Lily could think of such a wonderful surprise! Suddenly Maud loved Lily more than anyone in the world, even Amelia Earhart.

Maud pulled a red flannel nightgown off the rack and was holding it up to herself when Lily came racing out of the fitting rooms right past her. Maud ran after her.

"Lily! Hey, Lily! Wait up!"

Lily kept walking at a fast clip.

"Be quiet," she said in a low, strained voice. "I've got to get out of here." Her eyes scanned the store for the nearest exit.

"Lily, can't we buy some chocolate-covered peanuts? What's wrong with you? Are you sick?"

Lily kept walking. She was almost at the door when the store security guard put his hand on her shoulder.

"Is there something wrong with you, young lady?" he asked. "I couldn't help overhearing your friend. Are you sick?"

"That's not my friend," Lily mumbled through her coat. "She's my sister."

"What's wrong?" he asked again.

"It's the stomach flu," Maud blurted as soon as she caught up with them. "My sister vomited in one of the fitting rooms. I think she's going to do it again."

Lily made a horrible heaving sound.

"Oh," the guard said, removing his hand from Lily's shoulder. "Don't let me keep you. Hope you feel better."

"Didn't you want to buy something?" Maud asked as the store door closed behind them. Lily barely whispered something and started walking down the street.

"What?" Maud asked anxiously. "What did you say? I couldn't hear you."

Lily halted in the middle of the street. Unable to stop herself, Maud bumped into her. Lily's head slowly emerged from her coat. As she took a deep breath, her body seemed to puff up, like a cobra ready to attack. She had never looked at Maud like that before. Maud was scared.

"They didn't have it in my size," Lily said in a loud voice.

People on the street turned around to look at Lily and Maud. Lily's head disappeared inside her coat again; she turned and quickly headed for the bus stop. Maud followed behind, careful to keep her distance.

They found two seats together on the bus, but Lily didn't say one word to her the whole way home.

2

Life Without Lily

Maud was in the coat closet hanging up her jacket when she overheard Lily's bedroom door slam and the familiar click of it locking shut.

"Dinner's ready," Mrs. Moser shouted from the kitchen. Maud hoped her mother had made something good tonight. She often disappointed her by serving steaming hot meals. Maud had given up eating hot food months ago. It seemed too animated, too lifelike to eat. Even now, during the frigid month of December, she preferred her food stone cold. Mashed potatoes held their shape better when they were cold and cold meat never slipped off her fork. Maud walked to Lily's bedroom and knocked on the door.

"What?"

"Dinner's ready," Maud said in what she hoped was a cheerful voice.

"I don't care."

I don't care either, Maud thought, turning toward the dining room. She could already smell the hot roast beef.

Her grandmother was the only one seated at the

table. Her father was late getting home from the Small Animal Hospital, as usual.

"What's up, Doc?" Grand asked. She was looking over her lines for a production she would soon be performing in. She was an active volunteer with one of the local theatre groups. When she wasn't rehearsing for a role, she was sewing costumes or selling play tickets.

"Nothing, except homework," Maud said, collapsing in a chair next to her. She peered over Grand's shoulder, trying to get a glimpse of the script. Grand had been going to rehearsal almost every night for two months now. "Who do you play in this one?" Maud asked. Grand turned toward her and smiled, always happy to discuss her favorite topic—the theatre.

"I'm glad you asked, Maudy, because I think this production is especially interesting. I play Katisha, a wealthy Japanese lady who lives at the royal court. Acting in *The Mikado* is lots of fun. It's almost all singing, you know," she said, patting the musical script lying in front of her on the table. Maud looked at the title typed across the cover—*The Mikado*—or *The Town Of Titipu* by Gilbert and Sullivan.

Maud knew that Grand liked nothing more than to display her strong singing voice. She often heard Grand singing in the shower or in the kitchen when she was cooking something she especially liked.

"The dress rehearsal is only a few days away. I'm going to rinse my hair black for the part so I'll really look oriental," Grand said, pulling bobby pins one by one out of her large, circular bun.

"Can you make mine black too?"

"I don't see why not. Vegetable dye lasts only a few days, but we'd better check with your mother first." Maud groaned. There was no point in even asking her mother. She would never allow it. Maud watched Grand's white hair cascade in an avalanche down her shoulders and back. Instinctively she reached out to stroke it.

"Grand, can I brush your hair tonight?" She didn't think she would ever get tired of brushing Grand's beautiful thick hair.

"I'm sorry, Maudy," Grand said in a deep voice. "We're rehearsing tonight and you have homework, but you can come with me to the dress rehearsal on Saturday. If you went to the theatre more often you might want to become an actress. I think you have a lot of natural ability."

"I don't think so," Maud said, staring down at her place setting.

"Someday I'm going to have to get one of you girls interested in the theatre," Grand said decisively. "I thought Lily wanted to be an actress after she performed in those school plays, but she's at such a changeable age. One day she wants to be an actress and the next day, an archeologist. Acting is a commitment." Maud nodded wearily, glad that someone else had noticed Lily's chameleon-like behavior.

Mrs. Moser came out of the kitchen carrying a

large platter of roast beef with potatoes and carrots nestled all around it.

"Lovely," Grand said. Maud looked at the steam rising from the hot roast beef and groaned loudly.

"That's enough, Maudy," her mother said, putting the platter down on the table. She placed the backs of her hands against her flushed cheeks for a moment to cool them.

"We all know how you feel," she said. "There's some cold chicken in the refrigerator from last night's dinner if you want it."

Maud went into the kitchen and opened the refrigerator. The shelves inside the door were labeled Milk—Butter—Eggs, but what rested on them was an odd assortment of various colored bottles, medicine for the animals Dr. Moser was always bringing home.

Their last visitor had been Charles de Gaulle, a basset hound with a pacemaker, who followed Mrs. Moser up and down the stairs all day working up a heart attack. Maud would never forget the miniature poodle who had had an epileptic seizure in the middle of one of her mother's bridge luncheons. And she knew for a fact that there was no other person in the city who could prepare meals for a diabetic hound the way her mom could.

Maud poured herself a tall glass of iced tea to go with last night's chicken and cold Brussels sprouts. She popped one into her mouth as she opened the freezer and took out the banana-nut ice cream. She scooped it into two bowls, one for herself and one for Lily, just in case. Concentrating on keeping the tray of food level, she walked into the dining room.

"Not eating with us again, Maudy?" her father asked. He had just come in and was taking his place at the table. Maud smiled at her father and shook her head.

"Did you tell Lily supper was on the table?" her mother asked.

"Yes," Maud said. "She's not hungry. I think she has a headache." Maud couldn't count the dozens of times she had covered for her sister lately when she knew Lily wasn't feeling sociable.

"Are you going to keep her company, Maudy?" her father asked. Maud looked down at the cold chicken on her tray and nodded. It wasn't entirely a lie. She *wanted* to keep Lily company.

"That's very nice of you, Maudy," Grand said, buttering a roll. "Tell Lily we hope she feels better." Everyone at the table nodded in agreement.

"Do you know what happened to Lily's friend Suzanne?" her mother asked. "I haven't seen her in weeks."

Maud missed Suzanne too. She liked her a lot more than Lily's new friend Claire.

"Lily hangs out with Claire now," Maud said. "Besides, Suzanne started going to church after school all the time."

"She probably has Bible class," Grand said.

"What's that?"

"She's studying her religion."

"Why doesn't Lily do that too?" Maud was resting her tray on the table and nibbling on one of her cold Brussels sprouts.

"Your father and I have decided not to influence you in religious matters," her mother said. "When you're a little older you can make your own decision. Religion should be a personal commitment."

Dr. Moser nodded.

"Which religion is the most fun?" Maud asked.

"I don't know, Maudy, but I don't think most people choose their religion based on how much fun it is."

If there's a religion for flyers I'll join that, Maud thought.

A lot of Lily's friends were being confirmed and having bas mitzvahs lately. Sometimes on weekends when Lily called them they had gone to church or were at temple. Lily had told Maud about a questionnaire at school. She and Claire were the only ones who put a question mark next to Religion, and their teacher had asked in front of the whole class if they were sure they didn't have one. Maud wondered if Lily felt left out.

Just as Maud was about to leave, she thought this might be a good opportunity to ask her mother again about Lily's room. She hadn't mentioned it in two days.

"Mom, can I move into Lily's room?"

Her mother finished chewing a mouthful of roast beef, put down her fork and looked at Maud.

12

"I was hoping you'd forgotten all about that," she said. "I told you before, Lily wants a room to herself and your bedroom is perfectly adequate."

"It's the biggest bedroom in the house," her father added, his mouth full of potatoes.

"It gets a lot of light from its southern exposure," Grand said. "I think it's a very cheerful room. Don't you, Maudy?"

"I hate it," Maud said. "It's cold all the time. I'm going to get pneumonia if I don't move out of there fast."

"You were perfectly happy with your bedroom until Lily moved out," her mother said.

"No," Maud lied. "I never liked it." She knew that her mother was right. She had always loved her room until Lily left. Then all of a sudden it seemed dark and cold. Her parents had the ventilators checked to see that the heat was coming through to her room and even had it painted a warm yellow, but nothing helped. Ever since Lily moved out it seemed like the unfriendliest room in the house. Maud stood there listening to the silverware clinking against plates as everyone ate until she couldn't stand it any longer.

"I can smell dead bodies at night," she said in a desperate last effort. "They're in my closet."

Her mother's face screwed up as she swallowed her food with difficulty.

"Maud, stop it. Not while we're eating."

"How do you know what dead bodies smell like?"

Grand asked, a smile on her face. Mrs. Moser looked irritated by the question.

"I know," Maud said casually, and walked out of the dining room with everyone watching her. She put the tray down on the carpet outside Lily's bedroom and knocked on the door.

"What?"

"I told them you have a headache," Maud said softly into the crack of the door.

"Good . . . Thanks."

"Do you want something to eat?"

"No."

"Not even some cold chicken?"

"No."

"It's cold."

"You already said that."

"Oh." Maud tried to think of something else to say. "How about some cold Brussels sprouts?"

"No," Lily shouted. "Now leave me alone."

She doesn't mean it, Maud thought, sitting down in her usual spot opposite the door. She ate her chicken and Brussels sprouts quickly before the ice cream completely melted. She was sure Lily would want some.

"Lily?" she asked, wiping her mouth on her sleeve.

"Are you still there?" Lily asked in an annoyed voice.

"Do you want some ice cream?"

"No. I want some privacy."

"It's your favorite."

Just as Maud was about to say banana-nut, she heard Lily's footsteps crossing the floor; a record began playing loudly.

Maud sighed. This afternoon hadn't turned out at all the way she had hoped it would. She had thought they would get matching nightgowns and hold a secret Mount Olympus Club meeting tonight, just like the good old days. Disappointed, Maud ate the second bowl of ice cream and took the tray back to the kitchen. She could hear voices coming from the TV set in the living room.

It was the perfect opportunity to escape to her flying machine. Grand had left for the theatre and her parents were busy watching TV. No one would miss her.

3

The Flying Machine

She kicked off her shoes, tiptoed across the kitchen floor to the basement door and quietly opened it. She was the only member of the family who didn't mind going down into the basement. It was cold and dark, but it was in the basement that Maud kept her secret, her dream. Once inside she leaned back against the door and indulged in a long deep breath. She knew she was hooked. She was a basement addict. Something about the inviting smell of basement walls mixed with smells of old furniture stuffings and clothes soaking in the washing machine made her senses come alive.

Not wanting to risk being discovered, she decided to keep the lights off and began to descend the stairs in total darkness. She knew the way by heart. Fifteen steps down, around the corner to her right and under the staircase.

Maud's foot tapped lightly against her flying machine. Instinctively she lifted the blanket covering the waist-high wooden box that her father's air conditioner had been shipped in last summer, reached down to pull out her flashlight and a book and stepped inside. She turned on the flashlight and directed it toward the electric fan which she had placed on a stool in front of the box. After switching on the fan, she reached for the old ski goggles hanging from a nail on the wall beside her. Flyers had to protect their eyes from the wind. She settled down into the box by pulling up her knees and resting her book against them.

Maud turned off her flashlight for a moment and listened to the steady hum of her miniature single-engine plane. It was difficult night flying over uncharted waters. Not many had the skill to do it, but she was confident that she would make it safely to her destination. By her estimate, she would land in New Zealand by dawn and be fishing on an inland lake before lunch time.

She flipped the switch on her flashlight and looked at the book's cover—*Famous Female Aviators*. She had never known there were so many famous women flyers until she took this book out of the library. She had already read it from cover to cover several times, memorizing their names: Amelia Earhart, Jacqueline Cochran, Ruth Law, Bessie Coleman, Katherine Stinson and many others. Now she contented herself with reading over again the parts that she especially liked.

She had taken her father's library card and checked the book out of the library three months ago. Every time he got an overdue notice in the mail, Dr. Moser called the head librarian and insisted that the only book he had ever taken out of the library was *From Hounds to Heart Disease: A Veterinarian's Guide to Common Dog Illnesses,* which he had returned promptly.

Maud had decided to keep the book until she was a famous flyer. On the inside of the book's cover, in tiny print, she had already written, PILOT MOSER.

She closed her eyes and imagined landing her plane on the library's front lawn. She would walk confidently up to the front desk to return the book. The librarians would be so impressed that they'd ask her to autograph it and forget all about the late fine . . .

Here, in her private place, surrounded by the spirits of the aviators she was constantly reading about, anything was possible. No matter how much Lily ignored her or how badly things went at school, once inside her flying machine it was all systems go, clear skies ahead.

Just as she was beginning to relax, a small surge of panic rose up in her. She had almost forgotten the note. After school today, her teacher, Mrs. Obemeyer, had instructed her to give the dreaded pink slip of paper to her mother. "If I don't receive an answer from your mother by tomorrow, you'll get an F in English for this semester," she had said. Maud closed her eyes and breathed deeply to calm herself. She had the entire evening to think of something. She leaned over and shuffled through her books as though she might find the answer in one of them.

After she had been reading for almost an hour, the flying machine started to run out of fuel. It usually did around the same time Maud's legs started to feel cramped and her eyes tired from reading. She decided to go check on Lily. Maybe she had come out of her room.

Maud turned off the fan and went upstairs. After gathering a supply of Fig Newtons from the refrigerator, she stationed herself outside Lily's room again. The only new development was a cardboard sign hanging by a hair ribbon from her doorknob. It read: LILY'S ROOM—KEEP OUT.

She doesn't mean it, Maud reassured herself. She's just upset about not being able to find a nightgown in the right size. Maud was certain that Lily had the makings of a great poet. Only a poet would get so upset over something like nightgowns.

> Lily's nightgown didn't fit,
> She closed her door,
> She's in a twit.

Maud wished she had a pen and paper. She wanted to write that down and put it in her POSSIBLE POEMS box.

From time to time, she tried to look underneath the door, but she couldn't see anything. She pressed her ear against the door until it ached. Nothing. If she hadn't seen light coming through the crack she would have thought Lily had gone to bed.

She has to come out sometime soon, Maud thought. She hadn't had anything to eat all night and food was at least as important as privacy to someone like Lily. She loved to eat.

Maud was considering sleeping right there in the hallway when her mother tripped over her on the way to the bathroom and told her to go to bed.

4

Talking to Trees

Maud gave each one of her sixteen stuffed animals a light pat on the head as soon as she entered her room. She didn't want anyone to feel left out. She knew what it was like to be neglected.

The animals that lined the floor of her room looked like large pin cushions, each one resembling the next. Only Maud knew which one was a rhinoceros and which one was a buffalo because she had made them all herself.

While taking a personal inventory of what was available in local toy stores, she had discovered only large supplies of plush puppy dogs with black felt smiles and bunnies with pink velvet ears. At Grand's suggestion, Maud had set out to make her own menagerie of wild animals from pillow cases stuffed with rags and cotton.

Boris was Maud's prize creation. She made him from a long green gown her mother had thrown away. She had sewn on two pearl buttons for eyes and added pine needles and dried flowers to the stuffing so that Boris would smell as wild as he looked.

Maud draped Boris around her shoulders and walked to the bookcase to remove her favorite book on World War II airplanes, the one her father had given her. She opened it to the section on North American B-25 Mitchell bombers and pulled out a letter stamped with two small blood stains from squashed mosquitoes. She had been using this letter, the only one Lily had sent her from camp this past summer, as a bookmark. She opened the letter and reread it for the twenty-sixth time, studying each sentence carefully for a clue to her sister's mysterious behavior.

It was just the same the twenty-seventh time around. Nothing seemed out of the ordinary. Lily wrote about the one-hundred-mile canoe trip she'd gone on. She wrote about her bad sunburn and how the boys were calling her "Paleface" and "Freckles" . . . Wait a minute. Boys? Why would she bother to mention something like boys? They were everywhere, there was no getting around it; they were in school, on the streets, everywhere, like mosquitoes. Why bother to mention them?

Maud climbed up to the top bunk, sat down on the edge and slowly rolled her knee socks down to her ankles. Maybe Lily ran out of things to write about, she thought. The wool socks she had worn to school today made her legs itch. She scratched them until they looked like strawberry and vanilla ice cream bars. A good combination, she thought, jumping down from the bed to take off the rest of her clothes. She rolled them into a ball, threw them into her closet and shut the door.

Pretending that she was a kamikaze pilot, Maud started from the far corner of her room and took a flying nose dive into the soft billowing comforter on Lily's old bed. She rummaged around under the pillow for her pajamas, found them and slipped them on. She hugged her pillow and decided that tomorrow she would find out what had made her sister act so strangely in the lingerie department that day.

She was sleeping in the bottom bunk again tonight—Lily's bed. In the morning she was going to tell her that she'd slept in her bed and drooled on her once-treasured feather pillow. It had taken Lily years to get that pillow to a perfect squishiness. Maybe she would get so mad she'd come back.

Maud rolled over and looked out the window. Only a few weeks ago, red and gold leaves had flown like banners from the trees. She was glad she lived on a tree-lined street. There weren't many in the city.

Maud felt a poem creeping up from her toes. It often happened after she had eaten and was lying down alone in her room. Dinner had tasted like a poem, maybe it would sound like one.

"It goes like this," she said to the tree branches beating against her bedroom window. "Cold chicken, iced tea and Brussels sprout ice cream." Short and sweet. It didn't rhyme, but Grand said poetry didn't have to. It had a lot of pizazz. Besides, she was too tired to think of anything better.

Maud reached for the POSSIBLE POEMS box under her bed. She lay back and opened the treasured box with the dignity and respect this moment required. A roach fell out onto her chest.

The bug's tiny body felt like a ton of bricks. She tried to take a deep breath to calm herself. It was impossible.

"God, I'll do anything . . . Please make it dead."

Maud sincerely wished she had never decided to keep her poems in a roach box or that she had ever wanted to be a poet in the first place. Most of all, she wished the roach on her chest would disappear. It wasn't that she was afraid of insects. She used to race spiders against ants and drown the losers in puddles. But having a roach land on you unexpectedly was an entirely different matter.

Maud stared at it for what seemed a lifetime. Then she moved slightly and watched the roach for signs of life . . . nothing.

"Dead is dead," Maud said, almost too tired to care if it was dead or alive. She shook the tiny corpse into the wastebasket beside her bed and tossed her box of poetry in after it.

"This roach in my poem box has been a sign," Maud said solemnly. "I'll never want to be anything but a pilot from now on," she promised the tree outside her window. Maud shared a lot of important things with this tree. Who else was there to talk to when your sister had moved out of your room?

Maud took off her pajamas and reached for a T-shirt on the floor. She gave it a couple of good whacks for cleaning purposes and put it on. She wasn't about to sleep in something that had touched a freshly dead roach.

Glad that her last responsibility of the day had finally been taken care of, she felt for the magic boots in the bottom of her bed and pulled them on.

Maud used to have a lot of trouble falling asleep at night. Her mother tried everything from warm milk to bedtime stories. Nothing helped until Grand came to live with them. She checked on Maud the first night she moved in and found her wide awake, as usual. When she felt her feet, they were ice cold. Grand didn't do anything that night, but the following evening she presented Maud with a pair of boots. They were lined with rabbit fur and reached halfway to her knees.

When Maud stepped into them she felt magically protected, as though she could walk over hot coals or stand on nails. She was wild and dangerous in them and her father said she looked like a polar bear. Grand told her to wear the boots to bed. She did, and they worked like a charm. Once her feet were warm she went right to sleep.

Sure beats a glass of warm milk, Maud thought. She yawned and punched her pillow. As soon as she closed her eyes, she remembered the note her teacher had given her to take home that afternoon. It was still in her jacket pocket. She curled up around her pillow and tried to forget about it.

5

Cowboys and Buffalo Hunters

Waffles, bacon, eggs, blueberry muffins, milk and freshly squeezed orange juice covered the breakfast table. Maud sopped up the last bit of maple syrup with a piece of cold waffle. Smacking her lips loudly, she pulled back the kitchen curtains and looked around the small enclosed backyard for her friend, John Henry.

For almost a month now, he had been coming by early to eat breakfast with her. She preferred Lily's company, but ever since Lily had detected a small dimple on her left hip, she had stopped eating breakfast altogether. The only time Maud saw her sister was between classes at school. When Lily was home she locked herself in her bedroom or in the bathroom. Even when she dressed or undressed, she went inside the closet and shut the door.

What was she hiding, Maud wondered. Whatever it was, it had to be ugly. Or else why bother hiding it?

Suddenly the oak tree in the yard moved. No, it wasn't the tree—it was John Henry. It was amazing the way he blended in with the outdoors, like a pint-size Merlin the magician. He was standing very still, a snowdrift forming around his legs. He looked smaller than usual. He was clutching something in one hand. Maud opened the window and yelled to him.

"John Henry, what are you doing out there? It's freezing! Come in!"

"Now?"

"Now, John Henry," Maud said, losing patience.

"Shut the window, Maudy. You're letting snow in," her mother said. A gust of wind blew the pile of napkins she had just pressed and stacked into a sinkful of soapy water. "Hurry up!" Mrs. Moser shouted, but it was too late. The dried flower arrangement from the breakfast table lay scattered across the floor.

"It was stuck," Maud said. She slammed the window shut with a bang and walked to the back door to greet John Henry. Mrs. Moser opened a bottle of aspirin, took two and left the kitchen.

John Henry was wearing his cowboy suit, as usual. Maud looked down at his small, round face. His cheeks were windburned. A shower of shining blonde curls fell around his face. He looked like an angel, an anxious angel. He walked to the breakfast table, but instead of helping himself to something to eat, he plopped down on a chair and stared at the wad of paper balled up in his hand.

Just then, Grand walked into the kitchen. "Hi, John Henry," she said as she adjusted the belt on her red silk smoking jacket. It was a souvenir from one of the theatrical roles she had played. Grand picked up the bunches of dried flowers from the floor, stuck them in an empty cereal box and proceeded to start her day in the usual way with a piece of whole wheat bread, lightly toasted and buttered, and a cup of wintergreen tea. John Henry squeezed the ball of paper and opened his fist. Maud watched the paper expand slowly like a living thing.

"If I show it to Mom, she won't let me wear my cowboy suit anymore," he said. He looked as though he might cry.

"What are you talking about?" Maud asked. She took the wad of pink paper from his cold hand. It was an official-looking school note. She flattened it out on the table and read aloud—

"Mrs. Wilkes—John Henry has been doing very well in school, aside from his problem with circling words, but we're working on that . . .

"Are you still circling words?" Maud cried, looking up. John Henry blushed and looked down at his cowboy boots.

"Yeah."

"They won't fall off the page if you don't circle them, John Henry. We already talked about that."

"I know," he whispered. He didn't want Grand to hear.

Maud continued reading—

"This note concerns John Henry's costume, the cowboy suit that he is wearing to school every day. The other children are jealous and want to know if they can wear costumes, too. I know that you will understand my position when I ask that your son not wear his cowboy suit to school anymore.

"That's too bad, John Henry. Have you shown it to your mom yet?"

"No!" he shouted. A tear slipped down his cheek. He quickly looked to see if Grand had noticed, but she had left the room.

"Eat something, John Henry. It'll be O.K. . . ." Maud said, then thinking of her own note from school, added to herself, "It probably won't, but eat something anyway."

Grand walked back into the kitchen. She plucked the pink note off the table and placed a crisp, white one in John Henry's hand. Maud stared at Grand as though she were a genie. John Henry stared at the folded note. Maud couldn't wait any longer. She took it from him, spread it flat on the table and read aloud—

"John Henry selects his own clothes. As for his cowboy suit, it is not a costume. It is an important expression of himself. I would like to remind you of Shakespeare's famous line from Hamlet, *'Apparel oft proclaims the man.' I'm sure you will understand* my position.

Mrs. Wilkes

"Grand, that's forgery!" Maud said in something between a loud whisper and a shout.

"Nonsense. I'm simply pretending in order to help a good man."

"A good man?" Maud said, looking at John Henry as he spread peanut butter across a piece of toast with his fingers. "Do you mean pretending like when you act in the theatre?"

"Something like that," Grand said as she walked to the sink.

Maud sat cross-legged on her chair and started picking blueberries out of a muffin. She held each one in her mouth a long time, as though it were the last she'd ever eat. She watched Grand rinsing off the breakfast dishes. Her hair was tied back in one thick ropelike braid. Maud loved watching her do ordinary things in the same way every day. Watching her father shave in the morning gave her the same reassured feeling.

"Will you do it for me, too, Grand?" Maud asked.

"What?"

Maud reached into her jacket hanging over the chair and pulled out a pink school note of her own. She went to the sink and held it out in front of Grand. It flopped right under the running faucet.

"Oh, noooooo!" she screamed, cupping her free hand under the wet paper, hoping to catch some of the liquid words in it. Blue ink ran down her arm in a stream. Grand stopped it with her dish towel before it ruined Maud's yellow blouse.

"It's all right, Maudy. Just tell me what it said. Can you remember?" Could she remember!

"I can't go to school today," Maud said. "Will you tell Mom I don't feel well? Pleeeeeeease?"

"No," Grand said firmly. Then more softly, "Tell me about it. What did the note say?"

Maud traced the light blue stain up the inside of her arm and quietly spilled the beans.

"It was awful." She looked at Grand, who quickly nodded in agreement. "Mrs. Obemeyer asked us to write an essay about what we did over the summer. I don't know why she did that. It's already December. Everyone's practically forgotten what they did." Grand nodded. "Well, I did it. That's all. I just did it."

"What? What did you do?"

"I wrote about buffalo hunting. That's what I did this summer. I went buffalo hunting," she said loudly, in her own defense.

"I know you did."

"Well, I did."

"I know, Maudy. I know."

"Remember how I went buffalo hunting on Buffalo Avenue and in the park? There wasn't anything else to do with Lily away at camp."

"You don't have to explain it to me, Maudy. I know that buffalo hunting is a good thing to do when you're alone. So . . . What's the problem?"

"Mrs. Obemeyer didn't believe me. She said it was a good inventive story, but that essays weren't meant to be fictitious and that she would give me an 'Incomplete' for the semester and I wouldn't graduate or anything unless I did it over."

"Go get your books and put on your jacket," Grand said. "Oh, and wipe that peanut butter off John Henry's hands."

She left the room and returned four minutes later with a letter in her hand. It was written on her special stationery with her full name printed across the top in gold letters: Mrs. Maud Victoria Damisk Moser.

"Go on to school and hurry or you'll be late and there's nothing I can do about that. Give this note to Mrs. Obemeyer when you get there—and don't open it." She pressed the note into Maud's hand and closed the door behind them.

Maud was barely out the door when she carefully opened the envelope without ripping the edges and read the note—

My granddaughter is a buffalo hunter.
CASE CLOSED.

6

Claire the Bear

Maud watched as Mrs. Obemeyer read the two short lines in Grand's note over and over again as though it were a complicated mathematical formula. Tight-lipped and unsmiling, she looked up at Maud from behind her large wooden desk.

"Is this a joke?" she asked softly. Maud felt Mrs. Obemeyer's eyes studying her face in the same way as she had studied the note. Maud quickly shook her head, afraid that she wouldn't believe her. Mrs. Obemeyer read the note once more and then leaned back in her chair and sighed.

"Very well, Maud. You win," she said. "I'll accept your paper on buffalo hunting, but do you mind if I ask what line of work your grandmother is in? I presume she is a buffalo hunter too," she said with a sardonic smile. Maud shook her head.

"Oh, no," Maud said. "I'm the only buffalo hunter in the family. Grand is an actress. Last season she was just a peasant, but this month she's a rich Japanese lady who sings."

"Of course," Mrs. Obemeyer said, dropping the note into the wastebasket. "I should have known."

The school bell rang with unquestionable authority. Doors on either side of the hall were flung open, crashing against the walls. Girls and boys from six to fourteen years old pushed their way into the mainstream, their feet hitting the hard wood floor in unison. Maud found Lily and Claire in the crowd and walked down the long hall behind them.

"I don't want to talk about it," Lily said, walking a little faster than the rest.

"Great, just great," Claire said in an exaggerated voice. "I depend on you to look for a simple 'b' that we both need desperately for the secret ceremony and you don't want to discuss it."

Secret ceremony? The words sent Maud's mind into a spin.

"Nothing is simple about finding a 'b' in our size, Claire. Let's face facts."

"I'd rather not. Well, did you find them or not? I have a stake in this too, you know."

What is a "b"? Maud wondered. She had skipped her shower after gym class and raced all the way upstairs, hot and sweaty, to try to talk to Lily for a few minutes. She was going to tell her about drooling on her pillow and had decided to add that she had wet her bed, for good measure. She should have guessed that Claire the Bear would be monopolizing her sister again.

Lily suddenly stopped and turned to answer Claire's question. Maud, who had been walking on her sister's heels, not wanting to miss anything, almost bumped into her.

"Maudy! Get out of here!" Lily shouted. Claire clucked her tongue and rolled her eyes in disbelief. Maud blushed and started walking away slowly. She stopped behind an open locker and strained to hear more about the "b."

Another bell rang loudly, signaling the beginning of another class. The hallways quickly emptied. Maud peeked at the girls from behind the locker. They were covering their ears from the noise of the bell and making terrible faces at each other. She wished she were with them making a terrible face. She liked school more than Lily did, but not much more.

"I've got to get to class," Lily said. "Why don't you spend the night and we can talk about what we're going to do about tomorrow. Oh, my God, it's *tomorrow*."

Tomorrow? Maud was going to have to work fast if she wanted to be included.

"O.K.," Claire said. "Let's go shopping after school and then go back to your house." Lily nodded in agreement.

All at once it hit Maud. Claire spend the night? Lily always spent Friday nights at home with her, eating popcorn and watching TV. She was tired of sharing Lily with Claire. Friday nights were hers!

The girls started walking back in her direction. She jumped inside the locker and pulled it shut.

"What class do you have next?" came Lily's voice.

"Remedial math."

I knew it, Maud thought. She had always had a

feeling deep down in her bones that Claire was a dope: a dope and a homewrecker.

"What do you have?" asked the homewrecker.

Maud opened the door a crack for air and looked out.

"Romantic Literature," Lily said, raising one eyebrow seductively.

When Maud heard them going down the stairs, she came out of her hiding place. Their laughter echoed up the stairwell. The hall was completely empty now. Maybe this was how Amelia Earhart felt when her plane was lost, Maud thought. She stood for a moment in reverence for the famous pioneer of air travel, until her stomach grumbled.

It was the lower school's lunch shift. She turned and dashed down the stairs for the cafeteria. They put chocolate milk in the milk machines on Fridays.

Maud found John Henry in the usual place, the far west corner of the cafeteria. He had seen enough movies about the Old West to know that this was the direction in which cowboys felt most at home. Maud liked this part of the cafeteria because it was deserted. The lightbulb over the table where they ate had been out for several weeks, but that didn't bother Maud. She liked eating in semidarkness. That way she could spy on the other kids while they could barely see her.

"You're dining with a lady," Maud said, as she

plucked John Henry's cowboy hat from his head and placed it on the table. He ignored her and opened his brown paper bag.

"What did your teacher say about the note?" Maud asked.

"She said I can wear my cowboy suit, but that when I'm grown up I won't be able to."

"What did you say?"

"I said that I was gonna be a vet and I needed my gun to shoot horses with broken legs and my hat to keep the sun out of my eyes when I operated on cows in the field." Maud stared at him for a while.

"You're weird, JH. You know that?" John Henry nodded and took a bite out of his lumpy-looking sandwich.

"What have you got there, partner?" Maud asked. He laid it down on the table, lifted the top piece of bread and exposed broken bits of potato chips mixed with peanut butter.

"Mom didn't have any crunchy peanut butter left, so she put in potato chips." He picked several bits of potato chips out of the peanut butter and presented them to Maud.

"That's nice," she said, pushing his sticky offering away from her face. She couldn't imagine ever opening her lunch bag and finding junk like John Henry got everyday. No wonder he's such a puny kid, she thought. She always got things like chicken sandwiches carefully wrapped in wax paper and homemade cookies and fruit. Sometimes Grand stuck surprises in her lunch bag like cartoons she had cut out from the newspaper or funny poems she made up about food. Yesterday she had found "The Salad Ballad" taped to her fruit salad and the day before that "The Ordeal of Egg McSandwich" was tucked inside her egg salad sandwich. She had eaten half of it before she noticed it.

John Henry slapped the bread back on his sandwich, pulled off a small piece and gummed it a while before swallowing. Maud took a bite from her roast beef sandwich and watched a group of girls from her class eating lunch together at a table across the aisle. They looked as though they were having fun.

Maud had never really gotten to know any of her classmates. For as long as she could remember, she had hung out with Lily and her friends. Maud remembered one time when Lily had stood up for her. The older girls didn't want her tagging along anymore, and Lily had threatened to leave their group if they wouldn't include Maud. Boy, those were the good old days, when sisters were loyal and blood was thicker than peanut butter . . .

Now that Lily had changed, Maud knew that she was going to have to start thinking about making some new friends her own age. It wasn't going to be easy, but she couldn't hang out with John Henry the rest of her life. Being seen eating lunch everyday with a seven-year-old cowboy didn't do much for a girl's image.

"Are we gonna go again today?" John Henry asked, his mouth full of peanut butter.

"You mean to my dad's office?" It was getting so Maud knew what John Henry meant even if he didn't say it. She took another swig of chocolate milk and watched the girls across the aisle whispering secrets to one another.

"Are we?" John Henry asked again.

"I guess so," she said absentmindedly. "Meet me at the animal hospital after school." She got up from the table and went to the library. She had discovered several books there about flyers, and she liked to read for a few minutes during her lunch period.

7

Visiting Dr. Moser

The toilet flushed once, twice, then a third time. Maud emerged relaxed and radiant from the ladies' room. She always flushed three times in public places to make sure she didn't leave anything behind.

She liked the way her father's Small Animal Hospital smelled. It was a nice clean smell—something between dog shampoo and chloroform.

She walked to Dottie Luther's desk. She had been Dr. Moser's receptionist for seventeen years.

"Why do you always come racing in here and head straight for the ladies' room? Don't they have a bathroom in that school of yours?"

"Yes, but I don't like to go there."

"Yeah, she doesn't go at school," John Henry said. "She'd rather die. She'd cross her legs and turn blue before she'd go at school."

"Well, I think it's most peculiar. You're going to hurt yourself holding it in for so long. It's not good for you. You should eliminate frequently," Dottie said, guiding her pencil in one long fluid motion in front of herself to indicate the intestinal tract.

"Or you explode," warned John Henry.

"No. You don't explode, dear. You just shouldn't do it."

Maud liked visiting Dottie Luther and her father after school. She had started coming more frequently since Lily had changed. John Henry loved it here, too.

Dottie was wearing green beads, a green shirt and green pants. She was a well coordinated woman. That's what Maud liked so much about her. She was always the same. She wasn't changing all the time, like someone she knew.

Maud was getting impatient. She wanted to find her father, but John Henry had wandered off somewhere. She found him in the waiting room, seated next to a thin, helpless-looking woman. She kept inching down the couch away from him. John Henry looked as though he were deeply involved in a one-sided conversation with himself. The woman looked as though she needed rescuing. Maud walked over to collect John Henry.

"Don't you wish you had a lion like that?" John Henry asked the woman. He pointed to the picture of a lion hanging on the wall behind them. "If I did, he'd sleep in my room, go to school with me, everything."

The woman saw Maud coming and looked at her pleadingly.

"Leave her alone, John Henry. Not everyone wants everything you do, you know."

"Lions are different," John Henry protested.

Maud could see this conversation was going nowhere. Besides, she was more interested in the woman. She looked extremely uncomfortable. She kept shifting to a new position. Maybe she had to go to the bathroom, but didn't like going in public places in the same way that she herself didn't like going at school. Maud felt a sudden attachment to this woman.

"In case you don't know, there's a ladies' room right down the hall. It's just like a regular bathroom, not really public at all. It even has guest towels."

"Thank you. I don't need it," the woman said. She tucked her legs a little further under the couch.

"We *all* need it," declared John Henry. He sounded angry that the subject had shifted from lions to lavatories.

"Shut up, John Henry. We don't aaaaaaall need it aaaaaall the time. Where would the world be now if we all needed it all the time?"

"On the toilet," he said casually and walked off toward the examining rooms.

Maud let all the air out of her lungs and sighed as though she couldn't possibly take another breath after what she had heard. The woman coughed a dry little cough. Maud felt sorry for her.

"Do you have a dog or a cat?" she asked, more out of politeness than genuine interest.

"A cat . . . Actually, a kitten."

"What's wrong with it?"

The woman opened and shut her black-and-red

beaded pocketbook four times before answering.

"Nothing. Nothing's wrong with her."

"Then why are you here?"

"I'm having her put to sleep," she whispered. Her forehead broke into dozens of wrinkles. She looked as though breathing were suddenly so painful for her that she might decide to stop breathing altogether.

"If your kitten is all right, why do you want to kill her?"

"I don't. My husband wants me to get rid of Snowball." Her voice was shaking.

Maud made a silent vow never to marry. She put her hand gently on the woman's arm and whispered something in her ear.

"Really?" she asked, looking at Maud as though she were seeing an angel and the waiting room was really heaven. Maud nodded. She wished she could call the woman by name. She knew how comforting it is to hear your own name when you're upset.

"My father is the vet here and he never kills healthy animals. He wouldn't . . . especially a kitten . . . Even if you asked him to, he wouldn't do it."

"Like Snowball?" the woman asked. Maud nodded.

The woman studied her face for almost one full minute. She knew she had passed the test when Snowball's owner slowly rose from the couch and walked down the hall to find Dr. Moser.

When she returned to the waiting room, she

looked Maud directly in the eyes. "What's your name?" she asked. When Maud told her, she chuckled, said Maud was a nice name and left.

What's so funny about my name, Maud wondered. I go to a lot of trouble to make her feel better after her crazy old husband tells her to kill her own kitten and she laughs at me.

Maud had never liked her name. It was sleepy sounding, like Lily. She thought maybe their mother had been tired when she named them. Otherwise, they might have been named something energetic like Priscilla or Susy.

She heard the toilet flush. Dottie Luther walked from the bathroom back to her desk. Dottie was well named, Maud thought, noticing the small green polka dots on her shirt. Dottie saw Maud looking at her. Once again, she made a long sweeping motion down her abdomen to indicate the intestinal tract.

"It's important," she said and winked at her.

"I know," Maud answered politely. She didn't want to hurt Dottie's feelings. She just wanted to go home now. She shoved her hands in her pockets and sat down, waiting for John Henry to reappear. She felt for the list in her right pocket.

Today during math worktime, she had secretly taken out her dictionary and written down a few selected words that started with "b." One of them had to be connected with Lily's secret ceremony.

Maud unfolded a wrinkled piece of paper from her jacket pocket and read down the list—

1) Barracuda—Too hard to find. None of the pet shops have any.
2) Bat—No. Can't keep one in the house.
3) Bedbug—Itchy. Bad choice.
4) Beetle—No. Lily is afraid of insects.
5) Blackthorn—(a thorny plum) Never saw one.
6) Bloodsucker—No!
7) Blue Jeans—Everyone has them. Not special enough for a secret ceremony.
8) Boomerang—Maybe
9) Brunette—Maybe. Lily was always talking about dying her hair.
10) Bunk Bed . . .

That's it! Maud thought. Lily was always complaining about the bunk bed being too small. She had outgrown it. Maybe that's why she moved out of their room.

She walked down the hall to find John Henry and her father. They were sitting together on a small wooden bench in her favorite examining room, the one with old black-and-white photographs of airplanes on the walls. They were fussing over a white kitten that looked like a handful of cotton. John Henry held the squirming kitten high above his head as Maud entered the room.

"It's Snowball and he's mine."

"*She's* mine," corrected Dr. Moser.

"No, he's mine!" John Henry cried, pushing the

confused kitten into his right sweater pocket. He stood up, ready to fight for his new charge.

"We know the kitten is yours, JH," Maud said. "I think what Dad meant was that Snowball is a girl, not a boy." She petted the kitten's small white head. It bit her finger and clawed at the air.

"Be careful," Dr. Moser said. "She still has her claws and they're sharp as a hound's tooth."

"So are her teeth," Maud said, rubbing her finger. She watched the kitten crawl up her father's white medical jacket, hanging on by sheer determination with its razor-sharp claws. It teethed on his nametag and purred loudly. DR. SHEPARD MOSER was written on the nametag in block letters.

Dr. Moser reached into a canister on a table beside him and grabbed a handful of dog biscuits. He kept one for himself and split the rest between John Henry and Maud.

Maud studied an old yellowed photograph of a North American B-25 Mitchell bomber as she munched on the hard biscuit.

"Who was the B-25 named after?" her father asked. He was quizzing her. It was a game they sometimes played.

"General Billy Mitchell," Maud said. She knew the answers to these questions in her sleep.

"Where was he from?"

"Milwaukee."

"She's right, John Henry. Give the lucky lady a bonus high-protein dog biscuit." John Henry ran to

Maud, shoved the biscuit in her hand and ran back to Snowball.

Maud outlined the wings on the airplane with one finger, her thoughts lost behind the clouds in the picture. The glass frame was already covered with her finger marks. She especially loved this photograph of her father's plane. He had been a flier in World War II. Maud leaned back against the wall and slid down to the floor.

"You look a little tired, Maudy," her father said. "Have a hard day at school?" She nodded. Convincing Mrs. Obemeyer that she was a buffalo hunter had pooped her out.

"I'm pooped, pooped, pooped." Once was never enough to say something worth saying.

"Me, too," he said, snapping a dog biscuit in two and eating half. "Well, John Henry, are you eating dinner with Maudy tonight?" John Henry looked eagerly toward Maud. She nodded slowly.

"Yes," John Henry said, bobbing his head up and down enthusiastically. He popped the rest of a biscuit into his mouth.

"Don't forget it's Friday, Maudy," Dr. Moser said.

"I know."

Dr. and Mrs. Moser went out for dinner every Friday night. They referred to it as their Evening Out. For Maud it was just another Evening In, except that on Friday nights she and Lily were expected to fix their own dinner. Dr. Moser was giving instructions to John Henry.

47

"Fix a cardboard box with a blanket and put it in a warm spot so she doesn't get chilled by drafts. Don't forget to put newspaper on the floor until you get a litter box." Maud could see that John Henry was trying his hardest to remember everything her father said.

"Come on, John Henry. Let's go," she said. She stuffed three more biscuits into her jacket and walked out the door.

"Don't forget, John Henry," Dr. Moser said. "The most important thing is to love your pet. She needs you."

John Henry gently raised Snowball to give her a kiss on the head. The kitten purred sweetly until she was within reach of John Henry's face and then gave him a quick bite on the nose. John Henry walked hurriedly through the door after Maud.

"Come on, John Henry," she said, waving goodbye to Dottie. "Come on, come on, come on."

8

Friday Night
Means Club Soda

"I'm hoooooooooooooooooome!"

Maud ran across the room right into the kitchen counter, knocking all the wind out of herself. She turned on the faucet, bent her head under the running water and drank as though she had been marooned on a waterless planet for days. Those dog biscuits really leave you parched, Maud thought, licking the water dripping down her chin. She held her breath and waited for a response.

"I'm hoooooooooooooome!" she yelled again.

John Henry walked in the back door with Snowball riding on one shoulder. He put the kitten down and followed her around the kitchen, gently pulling her tail every so often. Maud picked up the morning paper from the table and gave it to him with the same instructions he had heard every time the Mosers took in another homeless animal.

"Here. Lay these down on the floor and keep the doors to the kitchen closed. The cat food is under the counter and you'd better get her some fresh water, too."

She took Snowball from John Henry and put her on the kitchen table. Snowball immediately stuck her head in the sugar bowl and before Maud had a chance to move had dipped her paw into a small pitcher of cream. She licked the sweet stuff off her paw and purred as Maud placed her in a box by the radiator. She quickly curled up into a ball on the blanket.

"You may as well give her this cream to drink. No one can use it now."

She left John Henry on his knees, spreading newspapers on the floor and ran upstairs to see if anyone was around. Lily was probably out with Claire and Grand often helped sew costumes at the theatre during the afternoon. Her best chance was her mother.

The door to her parents' room was open, but their bathroom door was shut. She ran up to it and tried the knob. Locked.

"Mom, are you taking another bath?"

"I'd like a little privacy, Maudy," echoed a voice from within.

"Everyone is always locking their doors around here."

"What are you talking about?"

"Lily's door is locked all the time and you're always locked in the bathroom. Nobody loves me. Can John Henry eat over?"

"You know I love you. Now stop saying that. I don't want to hear it anymore."

"Can John Henry eat over?" Maud asked impatiently.

"Now wait a minute. What's this about Lily locking

her door? She knows it's not allowed. Is she locking her door again, Maudy?"

"No." Maud would never purposely tell on her sister, even if she was ignoring her existence.

"Then why did you say that she was?"

"I don't know. Can John Henry eat over?"

"Of course he can. There are fish sticks and hamburger in the refrigerator. If Lily is locking her door, I'm going to have to have a talk with her."

"She's not," Maud said. She knew if this got back to Lily, she'd never speak to her again.

"I don't think you realize that if she fell asleep and there was a fire in her room, there would be nothing we could do to help her."

"What if there's a fire in the bathroom?" Maud asked, trying to get her mother's mind off Lily.

"A fire couldn't start in here. It's all tile. Anyway, there's plenty of water in here to put it out."

"Yes, but you *could* fall asleep in the tub and your cigarette *could* fall on the toilet paper and . . ."

"Enough, Maudy. Leave me alone."

She hated it when her mother smoked. She smelled cigarette smoke coming from the bathroom.

"Maudy?"

"Yeah?" She pressed her legs and chest against the door.

"Your grandmother won't be home until late tonight." Maud groaned loudly. "She's going out to the theatre and then for dinner with her friends. She asked me to tell you."

"Where's Lily?" Maud asked, her lips touching the crack in the door as she spoke.

"She called just before I got into the bathtub. She went shopping with that new friend of hers."

"Claire. For what?"

"What? I can't hear you."

"What did they go shopping for!"

"I don't know. Now, may I please have some peace and quiet for the remainder of my bath?"

"Did it start with a 'b'?"

"Maaaaaaaaaaud," she said in a final, you've-pushed-me-far-enough tone of voice.

Maud looked at the closed door. She felt she would explode if her questions weren't answered, but she couldn't afford to have anyone angry with her—not now, when she was getting along on a bare minimum of affection. It was a miracle that she could even function day by day. She thought of the fearless World War II aces soaring alone high above enemy territory and took a deep breath. She turned and courageously walked away from the closed door. Just as she reached the top of the stairs, she shouted so that her mother could hear.

"We have a new kitten! John Henry is laying newspaper down on the kitchen floor!"

A soft groan echoed off the tile walls in the bathroom.

"John Henry is taking it home with him tonight to see if his mom will let him keep it," Maud shouted. The groan stopped in midair.

Maud carefully lifted her skirt and sat at the top of the stairs. She gave herself a push, sending herself down the steps, landing with a loud thump on each one, until she reached the bottom. It was more fun with pants on. She didn't get rug burned with pants.

The bathroom door opened. Her mother appeared at the top of the stairs in her bathrobe. Beads of perspiration rolled down her face.

"I've asked you to stop doing that, Maudy. You're wearing out your clothes. I just finished sewing patches on the seats of two pairs of pants because of this little game you like to play."

"It's not a game. It's transportation, and I wasn't wearing anything out. I lifted up my skirt."

Her mother took a long puff on her cigarette as though she were thinking about a world problem. She pushed a lock of damp hair off her forehead.

"Well, you're wearing out the carpet." She turned around and walked toward her room.

"You don't love me anymore," Maud said, waiting for her mother to deny it for the thousandth time.

"I'm not even going to answer that. It's foolishness." Maud listened as her mother's door shut upstairs. She felt cheated.

When she returned to the kitchen, the floor was completely covered with newspaper. She wished John Henry hadn't followed her instructions so perfectly. She felt like yelling at someone. Lily wasn't home and her mother was being uncooperative. She looked anxiously around the kitchen.

"Why'd you do that?" she demanded, pointing to an ice cube floating in Snowball's dish of cream.

"To keep it cold for Snowball," John Henry said, touching the tip of the kitten's tail. Snowball was trying to lick the bobbing ice cube.

"Well, it's not good for her. She could get it caught in her throat and strangle to death." She felt better just saying it.

John Henry quickly scooped the ice cube out of the dish and popped it into his mouth. He started making sucking noises that irritated Maud.

"If Snowball touched that with her tongue, you're probably going to die. You catch diseases that way, you know." It worked.

John Henry's eyes widened. He opened his mouth, let the ice cube drop to the floor and waited to die. Snowball pounced on the ice cube and happily chased it across the room and under the table. John Henry forgot about dying and followed the kitten.

"What do you want for dinner? Fish sticks or hamburger?"

"Cow."

Maud didn't even have to ask to know what John Henry meant. He means hamburger because hamburger comes from cows. I know that kid inside and out, Maud gloated. She got the hamburger from the refrigerator and slapped it into two patties on the counter. Maud had never made the connection between hamburger and chopped-up cows. She thought of the large, stupid-looking, dirty animals she had seen on car rides in the country and decided to change the menu to fish sticks. Fish were much cleaner. They must be. They did nothing but swim around in water all day. Besides, she had read somewhere that eating fish makes you smart.

"Forget hamburger. We're having fish sticks. They make you smart."

She found them in the refrigerator behind her Fig Newtons. She loved her Fig Newtons cold.

"Brainfood," she said laying the fish sticks and Fig Newtons out on the counter. John Henry took a Fig Newton and ate it.

"Ask me something," he said.

"Why?"

"I want to see if I'm smarter."

"Not the Fig Newtons, dummy. The fish sticks."

He reached for a cold fish stick. Maud pushed them out of his reach, something a mother might do. The thought made her almost as sick as eating cows.

"Not until they're cooked, John Henry," she said and sighed. She wondered if her mother felt like this sometimes. She gave John Henry a glass of milk and told him to stir it with his finger until the milk turned to butter. That'll keep him occupied for a while, Maud thought. Lily had used the same trick on her years ago.

Maud enjoyed cooking on her parents weekly night out. She decided to roll the fish sticks in peanut butter and sprinkle the peas with cinnamon. John Henry suggested that they round out the meal with the dog biscuits Maud had saved from that afternoon. She gave John Henry his fish sticks warm from the oven and stuck hers in the refrigerator until they were cool. Everyone was satisfied—the meal was a triumph, as usual.

Suddenly they heard talking and shuffling outside the kitchen door.

"Someone open up!"

"Who is it?" Maud asked.

"It's me." She recognized the voice immediately and opened the door. Lily walked in, followed by Claire. Their arms were full of packages.

"We walked all the way home," Lily said. She sounded out of breath. "We didn't have any change left for the bus." She rested her packages on the counter and motioned to Claire to do the same.

"Do you want fish or cow?" John Henry asked, stepping out from behind the door.

"Who is this adorable little boy?" cooed Claire, patting him on the head.

"We already ate," Maud said, ignoring Claire's question. She had more important information to tell Lily. "Grand is out and so are Mom and Dad. Dad gave John Henry this kitten." John Henry held the squirming kitten high in the air for them to admire. Neither Lily nor Claire paid any attention. They were busy looking inside their bags.

"What did you get?" Maud asked, wanting to be included. The girls looked inside their bags, closed them, looked at each other and giggled.

"Oh, nothing," they chimed in unison and then burst out laughing.

"I'll tell you some other time," Lily said.

"We already ate," Maud said again, for lack of anything better to say.

"You said that. So what?" Lily dropped her coat over a chair. "Claire, let's just have sandwiches for dinner, O.K.? We can bring them to my room and watch TV."

"O.K.," Claire said. "Do you have any skim milk?"

Maud was taking a secret swig from the milk carton, as she often did when she thought no one was looking. She quickly withdrew it from her lips.

"Oh, God, that's disgusting," Claire said, pointing at her. "Do you have any soda, Lily? I've just lost my appetite for milk."

"Maaaaaaaaaudy," Lily said. "If you're going to spoil the milk for everyone, you can bring up some soda from the basement so the rest of us will have something sanitary to drink."

Maud didn't mind going to the basement. She opened the door and went downstairs, landing on every other step. She breathed in the musty dampness, loving the secret smell.

The beverages were stored in the fruit closet. She picked out two bottles of club soda, one for Lily and one for herself and a bottle of ginger ale for Claire. Club soda meant only one thing on a Friday night— there was going to be a club meeting.

Lily and Maud had started the Mount Olympus

Club together months ago. Maud was afraid that Lily had forgotten about it. She hadn't mentioned the club since her return from camp. It was Lily who had sensibly named club soda the official club drink.

Before going upstairs, she readjusted the blanket covering her flying machine. She felt better just knowing that it was here in the basement, waiting for her.

"Hurry up," Lily yelled from the top of the stairs. Maud ran up the steps and handed her the bottles. She noticed that Claire had left the room. Perhaps Lily had told her to go home so that they could have an all-night club meeting.

"Thanks," Lily said and then looked at the bottles. "Why did you bring up so much club soda?"

"You know," she said in a whisper.

"Not tonight, Maudy," Lily said, looking into her eyes as though she had just recognized an old friend. "Claire's waiting for me in my room." Maud tried not to look disappointed.

"How are you?" Lily asked. She looked as though she meant it.

"I'm O.K.," Maud said sheepishly. "When can we have a club meeting?" Lily hadn't heard her. She was busy loading a tray with sandwiches. She turned around.

"You can watch TV with us later if you want," she said and walked out the door before Maud could answer. Maud's heart felt like a twin engine aircraft warming up on the runway. That was the nicest thing Lily had said to her in a long time.

She looked down at the club soda and then at John Henry on the floor with Snowball crawling all over him. She was in the mood for a club meeting. John Henry will have to do for tonight, Maud thought. It won't be the same as with Lily, but it's better than nothing.

"Come on, John Henry. Let's go up to my room."

"I want to teach Snowball to play dead," he said, watching the lively kitten rip a hole in his shirt.

"Come on, John Henry," she ordered. "You're going to be honored tonight." John Henry looked up at her with renewed interest. "Tonight, you are going to be initiated into the inscrutable and holy Mount Olympus Club."

She grabbed two glasses and the club soda and headed for the door. John Henry quickly put Snowball in the box and ran out behind her.

9

The Mount Olympus Club

"The Gods of Mount Olympus will now come to order."

She tossed the leg of her mother's stocking over her shoulder. They both wore stockings over their heads, like caps. John Henry's skull appeared small and incandescent in the dim candlelight. His hair was flattened against his head. The nylon encasing Maud's head glistened.

"Drink it," Maud commanded. John Henry pinched his nose shut and gulped down the club soda.

"It's warm," he whined.

"You have to drink it. It's part of the ritual. The meeting can't begin until we do," Maud said, taking a sip. He was right. The club soda was nauseatingly warm. She had forgotten the ice. She reached for a book on mythology under a pile of dirty clothes.

"It smells in here," whined John Henry.

"What do you expect? It's a closet." She threw her sneakers into the corner and settled the book on her lap.

"My name is Athena, Goddess of Wisdom. Now,

all we have to do is find a name for you and then we can begin."

She flipped through the book until she found a male name. Zeus, King of the Gods. Lily had been Aphrodite, Goddess of Love and Beauty. Maud made the announcement.

"Zeus is king of all the gods. That's who you'll be."

She looked up to see if he was impressed by this great honor. He was picking his nose. She felt like kicking him, but remembered her position as Goddess of Wisdom and wisely decided to ignore him. She continued.

"Athena sprang from Zeus's head in full armor." John Henry scratched his head. The stocking was too tight. "She was Goddess of War as well as Goddess of Wisdom." He sneezed. "Her symbol was the owl." John Henry was holding his hand over the candle, watching the eerie glow it gave his skin.

"That's it! You haven't heard a word I've said!"

"Have too!" he shouted back.

"Then what's my symbol?"

"I don't have to tell. I know what it is."

"Why do I even bother with you? It's obvious that you're not Mount Olympian material." John Henry started to get up. She pulled him back down. "Do you want to hear something about your god? Would that make you happy?" He nodded. It seemed as if she spent most of her time lately trying to please everybody. She opened the book again.

"Let's see . . . It says here that Zeus liked to fool

around with as many virgin maidens as possible." John Henry burped.

"You're disgusting! Gods don't burp!"

It wasn't the same with him as it had been with Lily. She had given the club an air of dignity. When she had presided over the meetings, Maud had never been aware of being in a closet. Lily had made her believe that they were really on Mount Olympus, drinking nectar, in control of the world. Anything was possible. All she could think of now was how cramped she felt in the closet. She watched John Henry shifting around, trying to find a more comfortable position to sit in. Her forehead itched from the stocking.

"The club soda made me do it," he explained.

"Well, O.K., this time. Does the King of the Gods have anything to say?"

"I have to go home," he said, pointing to his watch.

"Fine. I have things to do anyway." She couldn't wait to get out of the closet and stretch her legs.

"Bye," he said pulling the nylon from his head. He dropped the limp crown into her lap.

"Bye." She blew out the candle, got up and closed the closet door behind her. Standing still for a moment, she listened to John Henry's light footsteps going down the stairs, through the back hall and into the kitchen. He must have been trying to teach Snowball to play dead because it was a while before she heard the front door slam shut. From her bedroom window she could see John Henry standing on the sidewalk in front of her house. Snowball was cradled in his arms. I hope Mrs. Wilkes lets John Henry keep her, thought Maud. She opened the window a crack and heard John Henry telling the kitten a story as he started walking down the icy street toward his apartment.

Maud wound the two stockings together into a small neat ball and threw them into the wastebasket. It was a mistake to have held a meeting of the gods with anyone other than Lily. She had a feeling there would never be another Mount Olympus Club meeting, not like there used to be anyway.

She heard laughter coming from Lily's room. Remembering the offer her sister had made, Maud walked downstairs. The door to Lily's room was open. She stood in the doorway, unnoticed, watching Claire imitate an actress they had seen in a movie.

"Oh, I do love you," Claire sighed as she leaned back on the bed, her chest heaving. "Do your will, Rodney." She raised her head slightly, as though she hadn't an ounce of strength left. "But be kind, Rodney. Be kind." Lily giggled. "We'll have to be quiet, darling. The child might wake up and hear us." Claire slowly raised her hand and pointed toward Maud.

"What do you want?" Lily asked.

"You said I could watch TV with you."

"You'll have to sit on the floor. There isn't enough room on the bed."

Maud went to the end of the bed and sat down on the floor. It was the first time she had been officially invited into Lily's new room and she didn't want to blow it. She tried to be as quiet as possible.

"Let's change into our nightgowns," Lily suggested.

"O.K.," Claire said. "I'll go first."

Claire took her overnight bag and one of her packages from shopping that day into the bathroom. She came out wearing a green flannel nightgown dotted with pink flowers and trimmed with lace. Lily took a similar package of her own into the bathroom. Within two minutes she was back, standing directly in front of Maud. The hem of the long green nightgown touched Maud's knees as she twirled around, showing it off.

"Like it?" she asked, looking at Maud.

Maud stared at the television set to keep from looking at the nightgown. She hated it. Lily's nightgown was identical to Claire's. Had she forgotten, like the club soda? Her own sister had betrayed her. Maud felt numb all over.

"Don't you like it?" Lily asked again.

Maud moved closer to the TV set, pretending to be engrossed in what she was watching.

"You know if you sit that close to the TV, your eyes will grow together into one big eye, like Cyclops," Lily said. She watched Maud closely for a response.

"I don't fall for that kind of kid stuff anymore, Lily," Maud said angrily. "I'm not a child."

"You could have fooled me," Claire said, giggling. Lily sat down on the bed behind Maud.

"Hey, Maudy," she said softly. "I'll let you wear my nightgown sometime." Maud turned around to see if she meant it.

"Can I try it on now?" she asked with uncontrolled enthusiasm.

"No," Lily said firmly.

"You give kids an inch and they'll take a mile," Claire said casually. Maud ignored Claire's comment and looked pleadingly at Lily.

"No," she said again. "You'll get it smelly."

"I'm too young to smell," Maud said loudly. "I don't even use deodorant yet." Claire burst out laughing and threw a pillow in Lily's direction.

"She's got a point, Lily." Lily reached around Maud and gave her cheeks a playful pinch.

"Hey, cut it out," Maud protested.

"I'm thirsty, aren't you, Lily?" Claire said. Maud saw her secretly wink at Lily. What was wrong with that girl? She was always thirsty. "Why don't you get us all some nice cold ginger ale, Maudy?" Claire smiled down at her from the bed.

"O.K."

Nothing wrong with that. Maybe things weren't so bad after all. Who cared about the stupid old nightgowns anyway? They were going to include her. That was the important thing. She decided to make buttered popcorn as a special surprise. Lily loved eating popcorn while she watched TV. No one knew that but her, not even Claire.

10

Before and After

She had thought of everything: ginger ale, popcorn (buttered and salted), Fig Newtons straight from the refrigerator and napkins. It was difficult walking with the heavy tray to Lily's room. Maud decided then and there to never be a stewardess. Anyway, she couldn't be a stewardess and a pilot, too. She stopped outside Lily's door and listened. Maybe they would mention the "b."

"Last week, Mom and I were walking along the street shopping for a you-know-what," Lily said. "And all of a sudden, she turns to me and says, 'Your breasts will grow, Lily. Don't worry. Before I had you and Maudy, I was small too,' in a really loud voice. Can you imagine?"

"Oh, God," Claire said supportively.

"A man walking ahead of us turned around and looked straight at me, you-know-where. Luckily, I was wearing a heavy sweater."

"I can't believe your mother said that in public."

"I wouldn't walk with her the rest of the way home," Lily said.

"I don't blame you."

"I felt bad about it, but I wasn't going to risk her saying anything more."

Unable to make sense of their conversation, Maud walked in the door. As soon as they saw her, they stopped talking.

"I made some buttered popcorn," Maud said. "It's still warm." She pulled the napkins out from her back jeans pocket and wiped up some ginger ale that had spilled on the tray.

"Great," Lily said, eyeing the giant bowl of popcorn. "Bring it here."

"Better not," Claire said. She motioned Maud to keep it at a distance. "It's fattening. If it was plain, we could eat it. But with butter, forget it."

"I guess you're right," Lily said hesitantly. "It makes me break out anyway." She picked at a small red bump on her chin.

Maud felt like drowning Claire in a pool of butter. If she hadn't been there, Lily would have eaten the popcorn.

"What are those?" Claire asked, pointing to the Fig Newtons.

"They're mine," Maud said.

"What's wrong with you?" Lily said. "Claire is my guest and she can have anything she wants. Bring them over here."

"They're fattening," Maud said. She set the package of cookies down on the bed in front of Claire.

"Well, one can't hurt," Claire said, taking a Fig Newton from the box. She popped it into her mouth.

Disgusting, Maud thought. She always took small bites so that she could savor every dreamy mouthful. Some people didn't appreciate the finer things in life, like Fig Newtons and B-25 bombers.

"This cookie's freezing cold!" Claire shrieked, rubbing her front teeth frantically, as though they were frostbitten.

"I forgot to warn you," Lily said between snorts of laughter. "Maud keeps them in the refrigerator." Maud watched Claire's eyes watering from the shock and smiled for the first time that night.

"Come on. Let's look at that new *Mademoiselle*," Claire said, obviously annoyed. She marched to the dresser to get the magazine. Lily picked up a glass of ginger ale and took a big swallow.

"This is warm, Maudy," Lily said, making a face.

It couldn't be, Maud thought. She had remembered everything; popcorn, napkins . . .

"You forgot the ice," Claire said, looking through her glass.

I forgot again, Maud thought. She could feel her face turning red.

"I'll get us some," Lily volunteered. "It'll only take a second." They all handed their glasses to Lily.

As soon as Lily left the room Maud looked at Claire's nightgown. What had gone wrong? She had worked her whole life being Lily's little sister and in one day, Claire had managed to destroy an entire life's work.

Claire was flipping through the pages of *Mademoi-*

selle. Her nails shone with red nail polish. She probably paints them to hide the dirt underneath, Maud thought. She never had that problem. She kept her nails neatly chewed down to the quick. Maud could feel Claire looking at her occasionally, but she didn't know what to say, so she kept her eyes on the TV. When Lily returned, she joined Claire in looking at the magazine.

"I'd do anything to look like her," Lily said, pointing to a magazine advertisement.

Maud got up on her knees to look at it. There were two photographs, side by side. In the *Before* photograph a woman was wearing a shirt buttoned up to her neck. She was frowning and her dark, brown hair hung around her face in greasy strands. In the *After* photograph, the same woman appeared wearing a tight, low-cut leotard. Her chest was enormous and she was smiling. Her hair was curled and it had changed to blonde.

"I'd be satisfied to look like the *Before* picture," Claire said.

"What happened to her?" Maud asked. "Does she have malnutrition? I saw someone all swollen up like her on the news once and they said she had malnutrition."

"Maaaaaaaaaaaaud!" Lily warned. "Stop looking over our shoulders and be quiet."

Maud sat down and read the advertisement about the bust enlarger out of the corner of her eye.

"Let's fill out an order form and send for one,"

Claire said. "If we're going to get our bras tomorrow, we may as well have one of these bust enlargers too."

Maud couldn't believe her ears. Lily wearing a bra? The word sent her mind racing. That's why they had gone to the lingerie department. The "b" had been a bra!

"Does your sister always stare like that?" Claire asked.

"Stop it, Maudy. You're being rude," Lily said.

Maud looked at Lily and then at Claire. Suddenly they looked like aliens from outer space.

"She'd better not tell anyone," Claire said, glancing in Maud's direction.

"She won't," Lily said. She gave Maud a threatening look. "Maybe we should just forget about the bras. I mean, what's the point? We don't have anything to put in them."

"You're crazy," Claire said. "We've got to get the bras before the baptism." She leaned forward on her hands and spoke with a slow intensity. "You wear nothing but a sheet, you know. And when those sheets get wet you can see everything and I mean everything." Claire folded her arms tightly across her chest. "That is *not* going to happen to me."

Lily pulled her knees up under her chin and nervously started rocking back and forth.

"What's a baptism?" Maud asked. She hoped they wouldn't think she was stupid.

"It's a big ceremony," Claire said. "A lot of people

come to watch you get pushed down in a pool of water."

"It's to save your soul," Lily added.

"Is it fun?" Maud asked.

"Of course," Claire said. "Why else do you think we'd do it?"

"It's even more fun when you do it secretly like Claire and I are doing," Lily said.

"Do you have to do anything special for the audience after you get dunked, like sing or tell a joke?" Maud asked.

Claire and Lily looked at each other and shrugged their shoulders.

"Do you remember what happened to Odette Obemeyer?" Claire asked. She was good at changing subjects. Lily closed her eyes and nodded as though she could hardly bear to think of it.

Odette Obemeyer was the daughter of Maud's teacher and a straight A student—that was all that Maud knew about her. She stopped breathing so that she wouldn't miss anything. Personal information about your teacher's family was invaluable. Maud's class had recently learned the definition of blackmail.

"I remember that baptism as though it were yesterday," Claire said, staring off into space. Lily uncurled herself and sat up as if she could hear better that way. Maud leaned forward and listened as hard as she could. She wished she had a pencil and paper to write everything down.

"There she was," Claire cried so suddenly that Maud jumped. "In front of the entire congregation. How many people would you say were there, Lily?"

Lily was silent for a moment. "Lots," she said softly.

"Millions," Claire said solemnly to Maud. Maud nodded. "There she was, naked in front of millions of people with a wet sheet plastered to her, no bra and a big grin on her face. The minister was so embarrassed, he forgot to bless her."

"Almost naked," Lily corrected. "Wet or not, she had a sheet on. I felt sorry for her."

"Poor Odette," Maud said.

"Poor Odette, nothing," Claire said. "She never buttons the top three buttons of her shirt at school, her chest is bigger than a grand piano and she never wears a bra." Claire rolled her eyes and leaned back as though that was all that needed to be said about Odette Obemeyer.

"The entire congregation was whispering and kids were giggling and pointing and . . . Oh, God, I'd kill myself," Lily said unable to go on. She curled up into a ball again on the bed. She pulled her hands inside the arms of her nightgown and yanked the hem down over her feet.

"She loved it," Claire said, swinging her legs over the side of the bed. "I bet she had it all planned."

"I'd kill myself," Lily repeated.

"Me, too," Maud said, mostly to be included in the discussion.

"Well, you've just convinced me," Lily said. "We've got to have bras before the baptism. So we'll have to get them first thing tomorrow morning." Lily looked at Maud. "You can come with us and bring the towels and hairdryer and anything else we'll need." Maud couldn't believe her ears. She looked around the room to see if she was in heaven.

"Good idea," Claire said. "She can be our First Maid and Chief Hairperson. All of the big movie stars have them and this will be our first major public appearance."

"I'll eat to that," Lily said and reached for the popcorn. Claire did the same.

"Hey," Maud cried. "I thought you were on diets." There wasn't much popcorn left and she wanted it for herself.

"We're starting our diets tomorrow, right, Lily?"

Lily nodded and split the remains of the popcorn between herself and Claire.

"Does this thing really work?" Maud asked, looking at the advertisement for the bust enlarger.

"Of course it does," Claire said. "It's guaranteed." She pointed to the guarantee.

"It's nine dollars and fifty cents," Lily said. "Do you think it's worth it?"

Claire nodded enthusiastically. "How much do you have?"

"Just enough for tomorrow," Lily said. "I spent almost everything I had on this nightgown." Maud perked up at this confession. Maybe Lily would decide to return it and get a nightgown with her instead.

"I don't have anything left either," Claire said. "I guess we'll have to forget it." They hunched over the advertisement with longing.

The movie on TV was over. Maud realized that Lily wasn't going to ask her to spend the night in her room, so she started piling dishes on the tray.

"Maudy!"

Maud tipped over a glass at the sound of her name. Fortunately it was empty. She couldn't have taken much more going wrong this evening.

"When you get back from taking the tray to the kitchen, I have to talk to you," Lily said.

Maud felt as though she had unwrapped a Christmas present and found exactly what she had always wanted inside. Lily was going to ask her to spend the night with them. What else could it be? Maud decided to go up to the attic and get out her father's old Air Force sleeping bag as soon as she finished with the dishes.

"O.K.," she said, hurrying out the door. The sooner she got rid of these dishes, the sooner she could come back and the slumber party could begin.

"Hey, wait a minute," Lily shouted.

"What?" Maud asked, stopping within earshot in the hallway.

"Do you still keep your money in that brown mouse bank?"

"Yes."

"Good."

Maud paused to see if Lily had anything else to add before she left for the kitchen. Why would Lily want to know about my bank, she wondered. Before, when she had kept her money in the glass piggy bank her mother had given her, everyone could see at a glance that she was loaded. She had watched her mother paying careful attention to her glass pig whenever she cleaned her room, polishing it to a shine. She had never seemed that interested in cleaning before.

That was when Maud decided to get the brown mouse bank. No one could see through it. Her fortune, accumulated from months of hoarding her allowance, would be a well kept secret. Pretty soon she'd have to buy another one. She knew this would cause suspicion. Only very rich people needed two mice to keep their money in. But when the first person came to her asking for money, she'd be ready. She had decided to say that she had gotten a second mouse to keep the first mouse company. She knew that she was still young enough to get away with nonsense like that.

Maud hurried to put the cookies away and rinse out the glasses. She was getting more and more suspicious. Why would Lily have mentioned her mouse?

On her way back to Lily's room, she heard talking upstairs. It had to be Lily and Claire. They were the only other people in the house. She followed the voices to her room. Lily was weighing the mouse in her hand and then passing it to Claire.

"She's loaded," Claire said, holding the heavy mouse in both hands. Lily nodded.

"Leave that alone," Maud said. She marched over to Claire and took it from her. She was too confused to know what to do or say.

"Maud," Lily said sweetly. She put her hand on Maud's shoulder. "I need a loan. Just nine dollars and fifty cents. I'll pay you back in three weeks. It's really important to me."

"I don't have it," Maud said, pretending to smooth down her bedspread. She quickly tucked the mouse under her pillow.

"That's a lie!" Lily said. "That mouse weighs a ton!"

Maud turned to face her. "That's because it's made of clay."

"Clay isn't that heavy," Claire said, fingering the lace on the sleeve of her nightgown.

Maud walked to the window. She needed time to think. Why was Lily so concerned with having a big chest? Everyone knows you can't fly if you're top heavy. She had never once seen a picture of an angel with a big chest. Maud looked outside. It was such a cloudy night, she couldn't even see the moon. She knew they were still standing behind her, waiting for an answer.

"Siberian clay is heavy. That's what my mouse is made of," she said slowly, not believing her own words as she heard them.

"Oh, Maudy," Lily groaned. "I can't believe you're doing this to me. My own sister. I've never known anyone so selfish. Just see if I get you anything for your birthday after this."

Maud's reflection looked back at her in the window. She wanted to give Lily the money, but she was afraid that Lily would end up looking like the swollen lady in the magazine advertisement. Lily was already beautiful. She was Aphrodite, Goddess of Love and Beauty. Couldn't she see that? Maud thought for a minute and decided to give her the money anyway.

"You can have it," she whispered. Nobody said anything. She turned around. The room was empty—she ran downstairs to Lily's room. The door was closed. She tried the knob, but it was locked.

"You can have it!" she shouted.

"Forget it, Maudy. It's too late. Claire is going to ask her mother for the money. Go away."

Maud walked upstairs to her room and shut the door. She couldn't remember ever shutting the door before. She liked to keep it wide open so she could keep track of everybody's comings and goings.

From her window she saw the lights of a plane moving slowly across the darkened sky. She decided that it was probably a freight plane on it's way to Siberia to pick up a shipment of clay. She wondered if she had enough money in her mouse to pay for a one-way ticket.

Maud decided to go to bed. She would need to be fresh and alert for the secret ceremony the next day.

She put on her nightgown, went into the bathroom and shut the door. She looked at herself in the mirror over the sink and once again tried to identify her hair color.

Last year, Lily had tried unsuccessfully to name the color of her hair. It was difficult because Maud's hair wasn't chestnut brown or coffee brown or any other ordinary shade of brown. Then one day when Lily and Maud were walking to school in the rain they took a shortcut through a muddy baseball field. In the middle of the field Lily announced her discovery:

"You have hair the color of this mud," she said. "The exact same color." Maud looked down at the deep rich brown mud oozing up around her shoes. Lily was right.

Later, when Maud identified Lily's hair as being the exact same color as scrambled eggs, Lily got mad at her. Lily liked to call her hair sun-kissed blonde. Somehow it didn't seem fair that Lily's hair should be sun-kissed and hers mud, but every time Maud walked through that muddy baseball field she knew deep down inside that she had something in common with it.

When Maud opened the medicine cabinet to get her toothbrush, she noticed a messy bottle with black liquid inside. It was the vegetable dye that Grand was going to use on her hair for the play. As soon as Maud saw it she knew what she was going to do.

She stepped out of her nightgown and leaned over

the basin. She poured the foul smelling dye over her hair and rubbed it in with her fingers. Some of the dark liquid dripped from her hair onto the white basin and ran down the drain.

Maud washed her face, brushed her teeth and whistled for a while, waiting for the dye to sink in. Finally, she took a quick shower and washed it out of her hair.

Her heart was pounding with the realization of what she had done as she stood dripping wet, only a shower curtain between herself and the mirror.

If Lily can change so can I, Maud thought, and with a sudden show of courage she whipped the curtain to one side.

She smiled uncontrollably at her reflection. She reminded herself of the *After* picture in Claire's magazine. Her chest wasn't any bigger, but her hair was a different color and she looked happy.

Maud rubbed her new black hair with a towel and slipped on her nightgown. Lily will like me better this way, she thought, putting the bottle of dye back in the medicine cabinet.

She walked out into the hall just as her mother came up the stairs, returning from the Evening Out.

"Suzanne, it's good to see you," her mother said, squinting directly at her. Mrs. Moser was a little nearsighted. "I didn't know you were spending the night with Lily." Maud giggled. When Mrs. Moser reached the top of the stairs everyone in the house heard her scream.

"What's wrong?" they all cried, running up the stairs.

"Maudy? Is that you?" Dr. Moser asked staring. Maud nodded and smiled proudly. She thought her mother looked rather pale. Lily and Claire burst into a string of giggles.

"The dye is cast," Grand said and laughed so hard tears were streaming down her face.

11

First Maid
and Chief Hairperson
Reports for Duty

Maud woke up ready to fight. Her fists were clenched and her head was tucked down. Today was going to be different.

As soon as she heard Claire leave the house she rolled out of bed, walked halfway down the staircase and sat on a step overlooking Lily's room. It was one of those increasingly rare times when the door was left open. Lily was in her leotard doing exercises on the floor. She and Claire had decided to start this morning regimen weeks ago in order to be in shape for their first major public appearance, the secret baptism. Now Maud knew the secret, too. Maud looked at the two new signs Lily had taped to her mirror—DUMP THE RUMP and BEAT THE BLURBLES.

"49, 50," Lily said, counting her last sit-up. She fell back on the floor, exhausted. Her face was red from the effort. Mrs. Moser came walking down the hall toward Lily's room and caught a glimpse of her perspiring daughter.

"Even God advocates moderation, Lily," she said with a smile. Maud watched Lily catch her breath before she raised her head enough to shout, "God doesn't have fat thighs!" Then came the familiar sounds—the slam of her door and the lock turning.

Maud sighed with disappointment. The show was over. She liked watching her sister work herself up into a sweat. It gave her a feeling of accomplishment. She had to call John Henry right away.

When she was sure no one was looking, Maud took the upstairs telephone into her room, its long cord trailing behind her, and closed the door. She took a flying leap onto her bed. It was piled high with layers of clothing and books. Her mother often said Maud's room reminded her of ancient lost civilizations buried one on top of another.

Maud spotted the tail of her boa constrictor dangling over the edge of her bed. She pulled all six feet of it out from under the twisted sheets, upsetting her books onto the floor, and wrapped the smiling reptile around her waist. She held its face two inches from her own and looked directly into its milky pearl eyes.

"Hi, Boris," she said and kissed its velvet head.

Maud dialed the number by heart. Making private calls from her bedroom made her feel like the president of a large country.

"John Henry, please."

While she waited for him to come to the phone, she hung her head upside down over the side of the bed. She loved to look at her room this way. The ceiling became the floor and the light fixture was a chair. Everything was in its place. Everything was spotless. It cleared her head. Maud was thinking of making a rattlesnake out of her father's old leather flying jacket and putting kernels of corn in the tail for a rattle when John Henry answered.

"Hi, Maudy." John Henry knew who it was without asking. Maud was the only one who ever called him.

"Listen, John Henry, you can't come over today. I'm going to be busy doing something really important."

"What?"

"It's a secret . . . . a secret ceremony."

"What kind?"

"Sort of a baptism and that's all I can say. I've been sworn to secrecy."

"What's a baptism?"

"It's when they dunk you in a pool of water in front of a lot of people."

"Why don't you take a bath instead?"

"It's not because you're dirty, John Henry. You have to get baptized or you won't go to heaven."

"I want to go to heaven!"

"Stop screaming or I'm going to hang up."

"Animals too?"

"What are you talking about?"

"Do animals have to get dunked to go to heaven?"

"I don't know." Maud heard him silently breathing on the other end, waiting for a real answer. "Yes," she said not really knowing for sure. "I have to go now. Bye." She hung up and went to search for some big towels for the secret ceremony.

Maud jumped off the city bus and ran to catch up with Lily and Claire. She glided past them on the icy sidewalk. When she reached the stoplight, she grabbed the post and twirled around.

This afternoon she, Maud Moser, had been invited to witness the secret baptism. Her mission as First Maid and Chief Hairperson was to arrange Lily's and Claire's clothes in an orderly fashion while they were being baptized and to dry their hair afterwards. Maud shifted the weight of her backpack. Inside was a small blowdryer, a hairbrush, Fig Newtons wrapped in tinfoil and two extra-large beach towels.

Lily and Claire joined her at the street corner. Together they waited for the light to change.

"It won't be long now," Lily said. "I just wish they had let us try on these bras before we bought them this morning."

Maud looked at the identical paper bags they held in their hands. DISCOUNT JACK'S was written in orange and purple letters on the side of each bag.

"DISCOUNT JACK'S isn't that kind of place," Claire said. "They don't even have dressing rooms. That's why it's so cheap."

"I guess they'll be all right," Lily said. "The package says, 'One Size Fits All' right on top." She opened her bag and looked inside.

Maud hadn't been invited to go to DISCOUNT JACK'S this morning, but she didn't mind. She had been busy looking for beach towels and packing Fig Newtons. The light changed and the three girls crossed the street. Maud was having trouble keeping up with their conversation as she walked behind Claire and her sister.

"What did you say?" Maud asked, leaning forward to see Claire's face better.

"Nobody said anything to you, little one," Claire said, looking straight ahead.

Little one? I'm the second tallest person in my class, Maud thought, but she didn't say anything. It was enough just being allowed to come with them. She didn't really expect to be included. Lily and Claire were walking ahead of her, their arms hooked together.

"I hope no one we know is at this church," Claire said. "I'd die if somebody saw us."

"No one is going to see us," Lily said. "We've never even been in this part of the city before. I hope we can remember how to get back home."

"I remember," Claire said. "I just hope the little one here remembers." Claire smiled at Maud and then at Lily.

"What do you mean?" Maud asked.

"You're going to have to find your way home by yourself," Claire said. "Didn't we tell you? Lily and I have to spend the night in the church, sleeping under the altar. It's part of the baptismal ceremony." Lily clucked her tongue and rolled her eyes at Claire.

Maud felt as if her heart had fallen out and was lying frozen on the icy sidewalk. She didn't know this part of the city. She only knew east from west by the fence in her backyard. That didn't help much in unfamiliar territory.

They had transferred three times on the bus and she hadn't been paying attention. She would never find her way home. A picture of herself crying in a police station flashed in her mind. She had gotten lost once before.

"Don't kid her like that," Lily said, giving Claire a playful poke in the ribs. "She got lost a few years ago taking the wrong bus home and ended up somewhere outside the city. Mom had to go pick her up at the police station in the middle of the night."

"Sorry, little one," Claire said. "We won't desert you."

Maud kicked a frozen wad of chewing gum into the street and forced a smile. She wanted to know if sleeping under the altar was really part of the ceremony, but she was too ashamed to ask now.

"Do you think that you can see through these bras when they're wet?" Lily asked. Claire shrugged her shoulders. As they turned a street corner by a Chinese restaurant, a church came into view. They stopped in front of it.

"Is this it?" Maud asked. Claire unrolled a piece of paper she had taken from her jacket pocket and checked the address.

"135 East 99th Street. This is it. North Shore Baptist Church."

"You'd think the daughter of a veterinarian would

be baptized at St. Bernard's," Lily said. Maud and Claire giggled and followed her up the front steps of the church.

Puddles of melted snow dotted the floor of the entranceway. It was crowded with mothers pulling boots off their children's feet and grownups greeting one another. Everything smelled like wet wool.

12

The Woman
with the Silver Arms

Entering the main body of the church was like walking inside an airplane hangar, Maud thought. Tall marble columns as long as the wingspan of a jet seemed to prop up the building. The mahogany pews were filled with people. A little girl ran down the center aisle, bumped into Maud, then turned around and ran back to her parents' pew. Her patent leather shoes made a light clickety-click sound on the smooth stone floor. A chill went up Maud's spine as the fearful organ music started, echoing through every corner of the huge church.

She was having difficulty keeping track of Lily and Claire in the crowd. She spotted them ahead of her, walking through a door. She pushed her way to the front of the church and into a long, empty hallway.

She found them in a back room where about thirty people were undressing and talking among themselves. There were women her mother's age as well as girls who could have been in her own grade at school. Several of them turned to look at her when she appeared in the doorway.

It reminded Maud of her school locker room,

crowded with girls dressing for gym class. Most of these women were as old as her mother—some were even as old as Grand. Maud had never seen so many half-naked women in one place. There were always separate dressing rooms for girls and women at the swim club she went to in the summer. At this moment, Maud was glad that she was still a girl. Grownup women took up too much space.

Maud squeezed past several of the women and went to the far corner of the room where Lily and Claire were huddled together on a wooden bench. She swung the backpack down from her shoulders, placing it protectively between her feet, and leaned back against the wall.

"Are all these people getting baptized?" Maud asked.

"These are just the women. The men are down the hall," a woman said, stepping out of her skirt. Lily and Claire were undressing, too. They whispered to each other and then burst into a string of giggles. Maud hated listening to them laugh when she didn't know what they were laughing about. Claire kept reaching into her DISCOUNT JACK's bag for her bra, pulling it halfway out and then looking around the room and dropping it back in again. Many of the women in the dressing room were covered with white sheets that hung to the floor. They looked as if they had been walking under a clothesline full of sheets and it had fallen down on them.

"Why can't you wear colored sheets with flowers

and things like the ones at home?" Maud asked. "Why do they have to be all white?"

"Because you have to be humble in church," Lily said.

"Yeah," Claire agreed. "White is about the humblest color there is."

You can hide a lot of dirt on a brown sheet, Maud thought, remembering the brown sheets she had selected for her own bed. Her choice had paid off. She never had to wash her feet before going to bed— even in summer, when she went barefoot. And in the winter, her rabbit fur boots magically hid her dirty feet from her mother's sight.

Maud was glad she wasn't going to be dunked in a pool of water with hundreds of strangers watching. Just taking a bath with a photograph of one of her Welsh ancestors staring at her from where it hung over the toilet made her embarrassed.

Maud felt a draft. There was a window behind her with a small crack in it. The afternoon sky was a grimy blue-gray. She couldn't tell whether it looked dirty because the window was covered with a film of dust or because it was going to snow again. She wrote "Maud" three times on the dirty windowpane with her finger as she listened to Lily strike up a conversation with an older woman. Lily was good at things like that, which was why she was so popular. All that Maud felt she was good at was daydreaming about being a flyer. She drew a picture of an old Curtiss Jenny airplane and a sun on the window and then turned around to look at the strange woman talking to her sister.

She looked about the same age as Grand, but that's where the similarity ended. She was wearing lavender lace underwear and about one hundred bangles on her large pale arms. Maud wondered where her belly button was under the rolls of fat. She wanted to ask if she was pregnant, but decided against it. She had asked a woman that once at one of her mother's bridge luncheons and it had turned out that the lady in question was just fat.

"Do you know where the baptismal pool is?" Lily asked the woman with the bracelets.

"Of course, dear," she said, lifting a white sheet off a hook on the wall. The army of heavy silver bracelets crashed together as she raised her arms and pulled the sheet down over her head. "Didn't you see the pool when you came in?"

Lily shook her head. The woman crossed her arms over mountainous breasts as she looked at all three of the girls. Her bracelets clanked loudly as her right arm met her left.

"Are you Sylvia Tillis' nieces?" she asked. Lily shook her head again. "I don't remember seeing any of you girls at our church services before."

"No," Lily said. "We've never been here before. My friend and I just decided to get baptized on our own."

"Well, bless your hearts," the woman said, throwing an arm around Lily and giving her a hug. Maud saw Lily glance at Claire and roll her eyes. "I hope you girls remembered to bring towels. The church doesn't provide them, you know."

"I brought towels," Maud blurted. She wanted some recognition. It had taken her most of the morning to find the giant beach towels they had used last summer.

"She's my little sister," Lily explained. Maud wished she had said younger sister instead of "little." It embarrassed her to be called little.

"How unusual," the woman said. "Sisters usually have similar coloring, but you have such blonde hair and your sister's is so black."

"She dyes it," Lily said casually. The woman turned to Maud, a shocked expression on her face.

"I only dye it for special occasions," Maud explained, knowing she would understand. Maud could see the inch-long black roots sprouting from her reddish-blonde hair.

"You should be undressing, sweetheart," the woman said. Her voice was sugar-sweet as though she were talking to a baby. "There isn't much time left, you know."

Maud hated it when people called her "honey" or "sweetheart." Saleswomen and waitresses did it all the time and now a half-naked Baptist woman. She couldn't wait until she was old enough to be addressed as Miss or Madam or even Hey, you.

"I'm not getting baptized," Maud said, looking at the woman's disappointed face.

"Why not? Don't you want to? Wouldn't it be nice to get baptized with your own sister?"

Maud looked at Lily's face for an instant and then down at the cracked paint on the window ledge. She scraped a piece off with her fingernail.

"She didn't ask me," she said softly.

"Who didn't ask you? What are you talking about?" the woman asked anxiously.

"Lily," she said slowly. Lily looked at her threateningly. "Lily, my sister . . . She didn't ask me to get baptized with her."

"Maaaaaaaaaaaud," Lily said, irritated.

"Well, it's true," whined Maud. "You didn't." She didn't like to whine, but sometimes it seemed like the only thing to do.

The woman threw up her arms in a gesture of helplessness. The white sheet billowed up, and for a moment she resembled an angel or a UFO. Her arms slapped loudly against her skin as they fell to her sides. The three girls stared in amazement. Everyone in the room turned to see what was going on.

"Nobody has to *ask* you to get baptized," she half-shouted in an exasperated tone. "God wants *all* of us here in this room today." A woman who had been listening clapped and another joined her. Maud didn't know whether she should applaud or not. "He wants *you*," the woman with the silver arms said, jabbing Maud on the shoulder as she said "you."

"I like your bracelets," Maud said, trying to change

the subject quickly before she was jabbed again.

"These bracelets?" the woman asked, extending her arms in front of Maud. Silver bangles covered her from wrist to elbow. All of the women in the room stopped talking. Everyone was staring at the massive arms encased in silver.

"I'm very proud of these," the woman said, skimming the palm of her hand gently over one bumpy silver arm. "Each one of these sterling silver bracelets represents a person I have helped lead to God— each one, a saved soul. Do you know what that means? Now think before you answer."

Maud could feel the tension in the room as all the women watched her, hoping that she would give the correct answer. She looked away from the silver arms into the woman's eager eyes. She was waiting. Maud wished Lily would answer for her. She would know what to say. But Lily and Claire were busy looking inside their packages and whispering to each other. She tried desperately to think of something to say and then said the first thing that came into her head.

"Do you polish them much?" She had forgotten what the question was.

The other women in the room laughed and started filing out the door. The woman whom Maud had begun to think of as Silver Arms gave a nervous little laugh.

"I don't think you understood what I meant, dear," she said. "We'll talk about it later." All of a sudden she seemed to be in a hurry. She gave Maud a quick pat on the head and floated to the doorway. "The sermon should be beginning in a few minutes." She peered into the hallway. "I think I hear the minister now. We'd better hurry. God bless everyone here."

A chorus of "God bless you, too," came from the remaining women as they followed her out the door, their long white sheets rustling. Maud listened to the sound of the women's bare feet slapping against the stone floor as they walked toward the baptismal pool.

The instant the room emptied, Lily and Claire ripped open their packages.

"I think that woman is nuts," Maud said.

"Who cares about her," Lily said. She quickly pulled her bra out of it's cellophane wrapper.

"This is going to be fun," Claire said.

In another second the bras were dangling from their hands, each with two cups of rubber stuck inside them. Lily and Claire looked at each other and groaned together. It seemed to Maud that they did a lot of things at the same time.

"Why did you get that kind?" Maud asked, pointing to the rubber cups.

"Shut up," Lily said curtly.

"They weren't supposed to be padded, Lily," Claire said, waving the bra in the air. "That wasn't what the package said."

"I know, I know," Lily said, collapsing in a heap on the bench beside Claire. "I guess we should have spent a couple of extra bucks and gone to a regular department store instead of DISCOUNT JACK'S."

"I don't know if I want to go through with this anymore," Claire said. "Rubber floats, you know. That's what they make rafts out of. With these things on, the minister will never be able to immerse us. The whole thing was a stupid idea in the first place. Just because everybody else . . ."

"I don't know," Lily said, placing the rubber cups over her chest. "I think they make me look kind of sexy." Claire did the same with her bra and they both started laughing.

Maud looked hungrily at the two laughing girls. At that moment, she wished more than anything that she were old enough to be Lily's friend, instead of Claire. She quietly unpacked the contents of her backpack as Lily and Claire continued undressing.

"We should fill these rubber cups with something," Claire said, adjusting the straps on her bra. "They feel funny with nothing inside them and besides, look." She poked one of the rubber cups lightly. Her finger made a deep indentation.

Maud quickly tried to think of something to fill the bras with. If she couldn't actually take part in the secret ceremony, she could at least contribute to the wardrobe. The only thing she had brought that was small enough to fit inside their rubber cups was the Fig Newtons and she knew they'd never agree to that. She decided to investigate the connecting bathroom.

There wasn't much to investigate—four sinks, soap, a towel rack and four stalls. Maud opened one of the stall doors and looked inside. She was glad to see that the toilet had been flushed. She hated it when people forgot to. The toilet paper was pink with a flower print, unusual for a public restroom where the toilet paper was almost always white. Toilet paper would be the perfect filler for their bras! Maud took out a roll and returned to Lily and Claire. They were still in their underwear looking around the dressing room for suitable padding.

"Here," Maud said, waving the roll of toilet paper over her head as she burst into the room. As she moved forward it unwound into a long pink streamer. "Use this."

Lily and Claire nodded to each other and started wadding up balls of toilet paper to shove into their empty bra cups. Maud was glad that she had decided to hold off suggesting they use Fig Newtons until she investigated the bathroom. She had a feeling she would never have been appointed First Maid and Chief Hairperson again.

Maud watched as Lily dropped a white sheet down over her head. Instead of lying flat against her body the way her long nightgowns always did, the sheet protruded from Lily's padded bra and hung out at a distance.

It upset Maud to see her sister this way. It made her look like her mother or Mrs. Obemeyer or even the big woman with the silver arms. She had never thought of Lily as one of them. Suddenly Maud felt like crying.

Lily was standing sideways and looking at her newly padded profile in the dressing room mirror.

"God, I really look stacked, don't I," she said excitedly.

Maud didn't think she looked stacked at all. She wanted to say that she looked like the same old Lily, only with two rubber cups on her chest and that she had seen fat boys with bigger chests than hers. But it wasn't true. Lily really did look different.

Claire pushed Lily out of the way, turned sideways in front of the mirror and pulled back her shoulders. Maud had never seen Claire stand so straight. Usually she slumped. Maybe that's what bras are really for, Maud thought—better posture.

Lily and Claire kept looking at their chests as though they each had discovered an extra arm. Maud thought the big grins on their faces were almost as stupid-looking as their bras. The whole thing was beginning to make her feel depressed. She could compete with Claire, she could try to understand Lily's changing moods and her locked bedroom door, but how could she deal with this? The longer she looked at Lily's brand new chest, the more defeated she felt.

There was absolutely no way she could be included, so she reached inside her backpack for her Fig Newtons. They were neatly wrapped in tinfoil. She took one out and ate it methodically, in mouse-size bites. Even her Fig Newtons were disappointing and they almost never let her down. This morning when she took them out of the refrigerator, they were nice and hard—now they were so soft they almost melted in her mouth.

Lily picked one up and popped it into her mouth. "Mm-m-m-m-m-m. For once these aren't as hard as rocks."

"I know," Maud said half-heartedly, taking another bite of her Fig Newton. It didn't even crunch. It just oozed.

"Come on, Lily," Claire said. "We'd better hurry or we'll miss the baptism." She leaned over from behind Maud and plucked the cookie Maud was holding from her hand.

"Hey!" Maud shouted. "Give it back. That was the last one!"

"Too late," Claire said, licking her fingers triumphantly. "Don't worry, my little fig. You'll be rewarded after the baptism . . . if you do a good job of drying my hair."

"Mine, too," Lily added, delicately picking up the bottom of her sheet as though it were the hem of an elegant evening gown. She walked carefully to the door and slowly turned around. "Any last words before we take the plunge, Claire dear?" Lily asked in a high-pitched theatrical voice. If Maud had closed her eyes just then she might have thought she was hearing the silver woman instead of Lily.

"Yeah," Claire said, stomping to the doorway. She

undid the barrette holding back her long chestnut brown hair and shook her head. Her hair fell to her waist. "Should I wear my hair soft and sexy like this or . . ." She quickly pulled her hair back again. "Severe, like this? Which style is better for a baptism?"

Maud felt tense. They would expect her to know the appropriate hairstyle. It was her responsibility as Chief Hairperson to know. She looked at Lily's hair to get some ideas. Two thin blonde braids dangled to her shoulders. Her bangs looked ragged. She must have cut them with her toenail scissors again, Maud thought.

Before Maud had a chance to suggest that Claire wear a bathing cap to keep her long hair from clogging the drain in the baptismal pool, Lily and Claire whisked out through the door, their white sheets flapping around their ankles.

13

The Secret Ceremony

As soon as they left the room, Maud wound some toilet paper around her hand and stuffed it down her shirt. She turned sideways in front of the mirror. The toilet paper slipped down to her stomach.

I don't look sexy, Maud thought. I look fat. She pulled the toilet paper out from under her shirt and used it to wipe up the Fig Newton crumbs on the bench.

She wondered when the girls would return. How long could it take to get dunked in a baptismal pool? Five minutes? There wasn't much time to get things in order.

She decided to first attend to her duties as First Maid. She carefully folded Lily's sweater and laid her skirt lengthwise on the bench to keep it from wrinkling. She arranged Claire's clothes the same way. Then she scooped up their jackets and hung them neatly on separate hooks. Each girl's boots were placed on the floor under her own jacket.

Both Lily and Claire had black boots, but it was always easy to tell which shoes belonged to Lily. They were the nice long ones. Lily thought size nine-

and-a-half was too long, but Maud thought Lily's feet were her best feature. Lily hated them. She said that on her eighteenth birthday she was going to leave home and have foot reduction surgery and that nobody could stop her. She was always talking about what she was going to do when she turned eighteen.

Maud looked around the dressing room to see that everything was in order. Lily's and Claire's clothes were in separate piles on the bench, and at the end of a row of lockers their jackets were hanging neatly on the wall.

Everyone else's clothes must be getting wrinkled stuffed inside those lockers, Maud thought. She was glad that she had thought to lay the girls' clothes on the bench. They would be pleased. But what if someone sat down on the bench without looking? Their clothes would be crushed. Maud carefully picked up the two piles of clothing and laid them on the floor next to the girls' boots.

Above the lockers was a large round clock like the kind in Maud's classroom at school. It was almost four-thirty. Twenty minutes had passed since Lily and Claire had walked out the door and Maud was already tired of waiting. There was nothing left to do. Her eyes felt heavy so she decided to take a little nap before they returned. It was going to be a long ride home on the bus.

She walked to the bench and lay down. The wood bench was hard and she needed a pillow, but her backpack would have to do. The beach towels cushioned the hairbrush and blowdryer inside. She closed her eyes and visualized the baptismal ceremony . . .

Lily was standing on a small platform high above the baptismal pool. She looked like a mere speck. The minister was treading water in the baptismal pool below, his long white robe floating all around him. He reminded Maud of a lily pad.

He looked up at Lily and shouted, "Lilian Smalls Moser, This is your life! Are you ready?" The speck high above on the platform nodded. The minister held a toy pistol up out of the water with one hand, while furiously trying to stay afloat. Breathlessly, he shouted to Lily, "On your mark, get set, GO!"

Bang! As the pistol went off Lily sprang from the platform and soared through the air, arms outstretched, white sheet flapping wildly behind her. As she landed dead center in the baptismal pool, a wave of water splashed onto the cheering congregation. Lily's head emerged, smiling. The minister and Lily climbed out of the pool. He shook Lily's hand and pinned small gold flying wings on her soaking wet sheet.

"Congratulations," the minister said. "By the power vested in me, you are hereby baptized." The crowd applauded . . .

Maud tried to shift to a more comfortable position. It was no use. The hairbrush inside the backpack was making a dent in her forehead, giving her a headache. She opened her eyes and sat up. She wondered what the baptismal ceremony was really like. If it was the way she imagined, Claire would probably do something showy like a back dive or a double flip. She looked at the clock. Only seven minutes had passed since she last checked the time.

"Thoughtless bunch, all of them."

Maud turned around and saw a woman standing in the doorway looking into the room.

"Were you talking to me?" Maud asked, standing up.

"I'm talking to anybody who'll listen. The trouble is, nobody listens."

She stooped down to pick up a dirty towel on the floor. The lines around her eyes deepened as she looked directly at Maud.

"I didn't do it," Maud said, thinking the woman was accusing her of messing up the room. The woman gave her head scarf a hard tug down over her ears and started sweeping in Maud's direction.

"Never said you did," she said, her eyes searching the floor for dirt. "It's them." She pointed out to the hall and leaned on the handle of her broom. "They're the ones who make the mess and I'm the one who has to do the cleaning up." Maud thought she saw the woman's eye twitch. "Cleanliness is next to godliness. Ha! Try and convince those people." She started pushing the broom furiously in long, hard sweeps.

Maud couldn't imagine having to clean up another

person's mess. It was hard enough remembering to clean up her own room. She looked at her neat piles on the floor and was glad she had gone to the trouble. She stepped out into the hall to give the woman room to clean in private.

Maud leaned against a cold radiator and counted the scratch marks on the floor until she couldn't stand it any longer. She had to see the secret ceremony.

She ran lightly on her toes up the long silent hallway toward the main body of the church. When she could hear the minister's voice calling out names and the sound of sheets rustling she slowed down and hid behind a pillar until she could see the altar clearly.

This is the best seat in the house, Maud thought, peering out from behind the colossal pillar. Behind the altar a small pool was sunk into the floor. A minister in a plain white robe was standing in the pool, up to his waist in water.

One at a time, people waiting their turn descended the slippery stairs into the water. Lily and Claire were at the end of the line. The minister announced each person's name to the congregation and asked some questions. The person then shouted, "I do" and was promptly dunked in the water.

Some people pinched their noses shut before going under, others bravely held their breath. They all came up with hair over their faces, but when they pushed it out of their eyes to see their way out of the water, they all seemed to be smiling. They looked refreshed and full of newfound energy. Maud envied them. She knew how invigorating a quick dip could be in the middle of the day.

"Florence Tasmain Pancake," boomed the minister. The woman with the silver arms lumbered down the stairs, smiling before her toes had even touched the baptismal water.

Maud looked at the spellbound audience. A plump, elderly woman sat in the front row; her expansive bosom was covered with silver trinkets, broaches and necklaces. She seemed especially happy. Perhaps she is the silver woman's mother, thought Maud, and wished her parents were here to see Lily.

The stained-glass windows enchanted Maud. They soared up from the dark wood pews to the distant ceiling, each one portraying its own story—like long, narrow islands of color and light in a sea of stone.

She wished she had a painted story window in her bedroom. It would have one airplane tailspinning down with Claire inside and two others flying straight up through the clouds carrying Lily and herself.

Suddenly, a burst of light flamed through the windows, bringing the colored-glass scenes to life. The sun had come out. She felt a thrill shoot up her spine, the way it did when she spotted a rainbow after a short summer rain.

She decided to run back to the locker room before everyone was baptized. She had seen enough and besides, she had to practice being Chief Hairperson before Lily and Claire returned.

The cleaning woman was finishing up as Maud burst into the dressing room.

"Where did you go off to?" she asked. "This is a church not a race track, you know."

"I know," Maud said, out of breath from running down the hall. As she fished around in the backpack for her hairbrush she wondered if the cleaning woman had any friends. She walked into the bathroom and shut the door behind her. Standing in front of the mirror she began furiously brushing her newly black hair in different directions. But north, south, east or west, it looked the same—short.

Suddenly, she heard doors slamming shut, one after another.

"Where is she?" a voice shrieked from behind the door.

Maud froze. The hairbrush she held in her hand dropped into a pool of water in the sink. I haven't done anything, Maud thought. She was terrified.

"Where is she?" screamed the uncomfortably familiar voice, louder than before. Now she was sure the voice was Lily's. A rush of fear swept through her body, leaving its mark on her face. She looked at her red flushed cheeks in the mirror.

"I haven't done anything," she whispered to her reflection. The doors kept slamming, sounding like shotguns going off. She heard the bench in the next room scrape across the floor.

Maud's feet directed her toward the door. Her

hand raised itself by its own power and rested on the doorknob. She felt like a mechanical doll. She watched her hand slowly turn the knob and open the door. What she saw on the other side made her want to shut it again. Paralyzed, she looked up into Lily's angry face.

"Where did you put our clothes?" Lily demanded. She was dripping wet. Maud didn't know what to say. She stood there, arms hanging limp at her sides and shrugged her shoulders.

"The joke is over, Maudy!" Lily screamed. "Where are they? I'm freezing to death! I mean it!"

Maud looked at the floor. The boots were there, but the clothes were gone. Claire was checking through the lockers in rapid succession. She looked frantic. The wet sheet was plastered to her body and her long tangled hair looked like rope. Claire turned around and slammed the last locker shut.

"Our clothes aren't in any of these lockers," Claire said. "I don't think your sister is very funny, Lily. My parents brought me that sweater I was wearing from England and it's expensive, really expensive." She glared at Lily and then at Maud.

"Did you hear that?" Lily screamed. "Now get our clothes. We skipped out of the sermon so we'd be back in time to dress and get out of here before the others got back. Now, hurry up!" She gave Maud a little shove.

Maud looked around the room. Only their jackets and boots remained by the wall where she had left them.

"I don't know where they are," Maud said softly. "I put them beside your boots. I folded them and . . ."

"I don't believe this is happening," Lily said. "Our clothes didn't just get up and walk away. Where did you put them?"

Maud looked down at the floor. There was a puddle of water at Lily's feet, her long, lovely feet.

"Somebody must have stolen them," Maud said, listening to her words as though somebody else had said them. She felt lightheaded, as if she had been suddenly transferred to another planet and was getting too much oxygen.

"Nobody steals clothes in a church, you little squirt," Claire said, shivering. She sat down on the bench and rocked back and forth anxiously. Her hair didn't look soft or sexy anymore. It just looked wet. "I'm freezing," she whined, rubbing her arms.

"You're not the only one," Lily snapped. "Get the towels," she grumbled and sat down on the bench beside Claire. Lily hugged herself to keep warm.

Maud's stomach tightened. What if the backpack with the towels inside had disappeared along with the clothes? She was relieved to see it on the floor where she had left it.

She hoped Lily would be pleased with the towels. Lily liked big ones, so she had selected the beach towels that they had used last summer. She picked up the backpack and gave it to Lily.

"They're inside," Maud said. "They're b-b-beach towels, b-b-big ones." She couldn't remember ever stuttering before. She sounded like a girl at school who stuttered whenever she talked. But that girl had *real* problems. Everyone said she was emotionally disturbed. Maud wondered if her sudden stuttering was a sign that she was emotional and disturbed. Her stomach tightened again.

Claire was hovering over Lily, anxious to be given a towel. Lily stuck her hand deep inside the backpack and yanked the towels out. Bits of sand flew out at Lily and Claire.

"I can't believe this!" Claire screamed. She picked a grain of sand off her tongue and wiped it on her underpants. Lily stomped toward Maud and shook the towels over her head. A light sprinkling of sand fell all over Maud.

"Why didn't you wash them?" Lily screamed. Maud looked down at the floor and ground some sand under her shoe. She rubbed her eye. There was a grain of sand in it. The more she rubbed, the more it hurt.

"I didn't know there was sand in them," Maud said softly. She didn't want to admit that she didn't know how to operate the washing machine.

"What the hell did you think you were going to find in a couple of dirty old beach towels!" Lily shouted. "Fish?"

"I can't believe this," Claire moaned. She took one of the towels from Lily and started shaking it out. "Come on, Lily. Let's get out of here before everyone gets back. They're going to expect us to donate some money or something and I've only got enough for the bus ride home." Claire took off her sheet and pulled two small wet balls of toilet paper from the cups in her bra. She threw first one and then the other in the direction of a trash basket. She missed both times.

Lily was sitting on the bench with a beach towel wrapped around her. A film of sand was sticking to her wet hair.

"Do you want me to dry your hair?" Maud asked softly. "I can get the sand out if it's dry." Armed with the blowdryer, Maud walked slowly toward Lily.

"No!" screamed Lily. "Don't come near me!" Maud stopped in her tracks. "Are you going to tell us where you hid our clothes or not?"

The girls would never believe her. Maud looked at Claire seated beside Lily. Her lips were almost blue and she had goosebumps on her arms. Claire was looking at her with more than irritation. She was looking at her with hate. Maud wanted to put on her magic fur boots, crawl into bed and sleep for a week. She had wanted everything to be perfect today, and nothing was.

"I'm never taking you anywhere with me again! Ever!" Lily shouted. Her freckles stood out like sunflower seeds against her angry red face.

Tears welled up in Maud's eyes. Everything looked blurred and wet like a watercolor, but she could still see the girls watching her, hating her. She felt the liquid build up in her eyes until, as if a dam had broken, tears overflowed and streamed down her face. She couldn't feel the grain of sand irritating her eye anymore.

"I hate you!" Maud screamed at the top of her lungs. She took a step forward. Lily and Claire sat up in amazement. "I hate both of you!" she shouted. The girls looked up at her as though she were a rabid dog. Screaming felt so good Maud wasn't sure she would ever be able to stop. "Your clothes were stolen and it's not my fault! Now leave me alone! Just leave me alone!" She walked past them and put on her jacket. "It must have happened when I was in the bathroom," she said, more calmly now. "Someone must have taken them then."

Claire picked up the lifeless sheet she had dropped in a heap on the floor. She gritted her teeth and pulled the cold dampness down over her head, then turned and walked to the wall where the jackets were hanging. The back of her sheet was streaked with dirt from the floor. She slipped her boots on and buttoned her waist-length jacket. The wet sheet clung to her legs as she walked toward Lily and Maud with a sour but resigned look on her face. "Come on," she said. "Let's get out of here."

"You're crazy if you think I'm going outside in the middle of winter in nothing but a wet sheet," Lily screamed.

"Shut up, Lily," Claire said. "You're getting hysterical. We have no choice. How else are we going to get home? Wrapped in toilet paper?" Lily sat silently for a moment and then stood up and put on her boots and jacket.

Maud walked down the empty hallway behind Lily and Claire, her backpack balanced on one shoulder. It was much smaller without the beach towels inside. She had left them in the dressing room. She never wanted to see them again.

"Great," Lily said. "Just great. We have to be seen like this in public. If anyone I know sees me I'm going to ask Mother if I can change schools."

"I just hope they let us on the bus," Claire said as they turned a street corner. She gathered her long wet hair in one hand and stuck it down the back of her jacket. "You know people are going to think our hair is greasy," she said.

"It's not greasy," Lily said. "It's wet. Anyone can see that." Maud looked around. Luckily there was no one waiting at the bus stop.

"*I* know it's wet," Claire said. "And *you* know it's wet, but that's not what they're going to think. They'll think we're student nuns wearing long white gowns and we're wet because we got thrown in a snowbank by a gang of atheist kids or something and our hair is disgustingly greasy because we're practicing humility and wouldn't do anything vain like washing it."

"Nuns wash their hair," Lily stated matter-of-factly. Claire shook her head again and they continued their argument, but Maud couldn't hear them talking anymore.

A bus had stopped and Lily and Claire had gotten on. Maud followed them to the back of the bus where she saw three empty seats in a row. Just as she was about to sit down Claire grabbed her backpack and placed it on the remaining seat.

"Sorry, this seat is taken," Claire said. Maud looked at Lily to see what she would do, but Lily was knocking the water out of her ears and looking out the window, lost in another world.

The only other available seat in the bus was located next to a young woman holding a baby. The baby was making noises as if it were getting ready to vomit. Maud sat down and hoped for the best.

14

The Mysterious Disappearance of Lily's Cake

Home at last. As Maud stomped the snow off her boots on the front doormat she heard Lily's bedroom door slam shut. She thought briefly about sitting outside her door and then decided against it. Why bother? She never knows I'm there anyway, Maud thought.

"What's going on down there?" Grand shouted from the top of the staircase.

"Nothing," Maud said. She could hear Grand coming down the steps. She turned around. Standing before her was a bizarre looking woman wearing a blue silk kimono that reached to the floor. With horror she realized that this stranger was her own Grand. Her face was covered with a kaleidoscope of colors and her hair wasn't white anymore.

"Like it?" Grand asked, twirling around in the same way Lily had in her new nightgown the evening before. The wide sleeves of her costume billowed up into the air as she raised her arms and spun around one more time. The ends of her long black hair hit Maud in the face.

"It's my costume for the play and this is my oriental stage makeup." Grand leaned over and put her strange new face directly in front of Maud's. Thick slashes of black lined her eyes, making them seem to slant up. It was scary seeing her like this.

"I don't like it," Maud said. "You don't look like you." It was bad enough having Lily change every day without having Grand change too.

"I don't want to look like me," Grand said. "That's the whole point. I'm a Japanese lady. The dress rehearsal for *The Mikado* is tonight."

"Your hair," Maud said, pointing to the long black tresses dangling to Grand's waist.

"Yes," she said pulling it back. "Striking, isn't it? I think it will show up very well on stage. For a few days you and I will have the same hair color, Maudy. The color in your hair will rinse out soon, but until then people may think we're sisters. What do you think?" She laughed.

Maud didn't know what to think. Grand wasn't her sister. Lily was. What was wrong with everyone? Didn't they know who they were anymore?

"I'll put some stage makeup on you sometime, Maudy. We'll change you into a clown or a queen or anything you like. Every actress should learn how to apply her own makeup." Maud wished Grand would stop talking about being an actress.

"Can you make me look like Amelia Earhart?" she asked.

"Why would I want to do that?" Grand asked, lifting the hem of her silk kimono and looking at the gold sandals on her feet. Maud was startled to see that she had painted her toenails gold too. Maud couldn't believe her ears.

"Because she's a famous flier," she said, almost shouting.

"That's nice," Grand said, making different faces in the hall mirror. One moment she looked joyously happy and the next, her face was veiled with anger. Before a performance Grand always seemed a bit preoccupied.

"Can you make me look like Amelia Earhart?" Maud asked again, determined to salvage what was left of a miserable afternoon.

"I'm sorry, Maudy. Not today. I have to go to the dress rehearsal. Would you like to come along? You'll have a front row seat."

"No thanks" Maud said, disappointed. She had hoped Grand would be home to keep her company tonight. She shuffled off toward the kitchen wondering if there were any Fig Newtons left in the refrigerator. They might lift her spirits.

Mrs. Moser was putting away clean dishes and Dr. Moser was hammering a nail into a small wood box. Maud joined her father at the kitchen table.

"I'm the only one around here who knows who they are," she said.

"Where's Lily?" her mother asked as though she hadn't heard a word Maud had said.

"She's in her room . . . She got baptized today," Maud blurted. There, she had done it. She'd told on

Lily and she didn't care. She hoped her parents dragged Lily out to the living room in her wet sheet and made her confess. After all Lily had put her through today she wouldn't care if they locked her in her room for a week. Maud noticed her parents looking at her, waiting for an explanation. She shrugged her shoulders.

"I don't know why she did it," Maud said. "I think she's going crazy."

"Don't be silly, Maudy," her mother said as she separated the forks from the spoons. "If that's what she wants to do, I think it's just fine. When she's ready to talk about it I'm sure she'll tell us all about it herself. Don't you think so, dear?" She looked at Dr. Moser. He was nibbling on a handful of what looked like seeds.

"Why not?" he mumbled, his mouth still full. "I can't see that it will do her any harm."

"You wouldn't say that if you had been there," Maud said, irritated that her parents weren't the least bit angry with Lily. "She took off all her clothes and put on a sheet and they dunked her under water in front of millions of people."

"Your father and I have been to baptisms before, Maudy. We know what happens."

Maud felt like screaming. Instead, she reached into the bowl of seeds her father was eating and swallowed an entire handful.

"What are these? Sesame seeds?"

"Actually, it's bird seed," he said matter-of-factly.

"Do you like the bird house I'm making?" He turned the wood box around to show the small hole in front.

He's always the same, thought Maud, building bird houses in the winter, shining snow shovels in the summer. She didn't know whether it was the bird seed or her father, but she felt a bit calmer.

"Nice, Dad." She held up the bird house and inspected each side to show her approval. "Do you think the birds will be able to fit through that hole, though? I mean, how wide is the average bird's wingspread?"

"Birds! Airplanes! You've heard me say it once, but I'll say it again," her mother said. "If God had meant man to fly he'd have given him wings."

"I don't care whether men fly," Maud said. "But I'm going to."

"You're probably right," Dr. Moser said. "Perhaps only birds and young girls were meant to fly and the rest of us should be content with long drives in the country." He winked at her. "You see the Curtiss Jenny this afternoon, Maudy?"

"What a darling name," Mrs. Moser said. "Is she a new friend of yours, Maudy?"

Maud rolled her eyes in exasperation as her father patiently explained.

"Curtiss Jenny is an airplane, dear—a World War I military training plane."

"Where did you spot it?" Maud asked, excitedly tugging on her father's sleeve.

"It went right over our backyard this afternoon. They were having an antique air show not far from here today. The Curtiss must have been on its way there. It was flying so low I could almost touch it. Where were you?"

"With Lily," Maud said, fuming with anger.

"Oh, that's right," her father said. "At the baptism. Too bad. We could have gone to the air show if you had been home." He went back to his bird house.

Not only had Lily accused Maud of stealing her clothes today, but she was also responsible for her missing what could have been the most spectacular sight of her lifetime.

"I could kill her," Maud muttered under her breath.

"Did you say something, Maudy?" her mother asked. Maud shook her head. She got up and lifted a long, clean blunt-edged knife off the kitchen counter. She tucked the knife under her arm and headed for the basement.

"Where are you taking that knife?" her mother asked.

"I need it for a class assignment," Maud lied. "It's too complicated to explain."

"All right. Just be sure that it's put back in this drawer when you're through using it." Maud nodded. As she was about to go down the steps she heard her mother calling her back.

"Maudy, I'd like you to wash the cucumbers in the sink for our salad tonight." They had been having giant cucumber salads every night for a week. Mom must be starting another diet, Maud thought.

"I'll do it later, Mom."

"Now, Maudy. I'd like it done before you start on your school project. Dinner will be ready in half an hour. Until then I'm going upstairs for a little peace and quiet."

Peace and quiet could mean only one thing. Another bath. She sure does like being clean, Maud thought, watching her mother leave the kitchen.

"Have a nice bath," Maud shouted, grateful that her mother hadn't inquired further into the nature of her class assignment. Maud picked up the two cucumbers in the sink, glanced at her father who was busy sanding down the edges on his bird house and quickly dropped the cucumbers into the dishwasher. She closed its door and pressed the wash button. Weapon in hand, she walked past her father to the basement door.

She held the table knife, point down in front of her, like a mighty sword, slicing her way through the cool damp basement air as she went down the stairs.

The whole day seemed like one long tailspin down and here she was in the basement, as far down as a person could get without digging a hole—and she was still tailspinning. She imagined putting on a parachute and bailing out of her plane, enjoying the heavenly feeling of floating down to earth and safety.

She walked to the familiar alcove under the staircase and climbed inside her flying machine. As soon as she sat down she realized that it wasn't going to work this time. She couldn't escape from the memory of this disastrous afternoon.

It's all Lily's fault, Maud thought. All she ever does is think of herself. Ever since she came back from camp this summer my life has been horrible. Ever since she decided to be a grownup, she stopped being a sister. She's as bad as Claire.

Maud visualized Lily's angry face as she accused her of hiding their clothes. The same fury she had known this afternoon rose up in her again. Suddenly she jumped up in her flying machine and made an announcement to her companion aviator spirits in the basement.

"She's gonna get it!"

Maud stepped out of the flying machine, knife in hand and marched to the far corner of the basement. Her flashlight shone on the handle of the big old freezer. Her mother didn't use it for much anymore since she had gotten the new one upstairs. This freezer held only big things like Thanksgiving turkeys, giant bags of ice and desserts Mrs. Moser wanted to save for special occasions. She knew that if she kept cakes or pies in the freezer upstairs they would be eaten before the special occasion arose, so she hid them in the old freezer.

Maud had made it her business to know all of her mother's hiding places. She happened to know that ever since last Tuesday afternoon, the basement (specifically the freezer), had housed one extra-large chocolate cake with yellow and white flowers and the words, HAPPY BIRTHDAY LILY written in icing on top. She had also been secretly informed by a reliable source (Grand), that this impressive dessert was to be unfrozen and served to the entire Moser household at a birthday celebration for a Miss Lilian Smalls Moser (commonly known as Lily), due to the fact that Miss Moser had been ill on the anniversary of her birth. The family had postponed the celebration of the joyous event until next weekend.

It is a well known fact that Miss Lilian Moser's favorite flavor is chocolate.

It is also a well known fact, Maud thought, that Lily is an ungrateful creep with a wonderful younger sister whose favorite flavor is also chocolate and that Lily Moser will be eating Jell-O on her birthday due to the mysterious disappearance of her cake.

When Maud opened the freezer door the inside lit up. There sat the most magnificent cake she had ever seen, bigger than any birthday cake anyone in the family had ever had. Maud could only assume that her mother thought significantly more of Lily than she did of herself.

Maud clearly remembered her disappointment last year at her birthday dinner when her mother had placed a small white cake in front of her on the table. When she had told her mother that she wanted a cake that was different, she hadn't expected something like that. It was sprinkled with coconut. It was the first time Maud had ever tasted the exotic sweetness of coconut. She hated it. That day she decided to never trust her mother's judgment in selecting birthday cakes again. Lily had been smart to pick out her own cake.

Maud tapped Lily's frozen cake with her knife. It clinked against the icing. She knocked it with her fist—hard as a rock. She lifted the cake out of the freezer and placed it on the floor. It took her a few minutes to chisel away a piece. It was so cold she had to throw it up and down like a hot potato until it started to thaw. When the icing began to stick to her fingers, she decided it had thawed out enough. She took a bite. As soon as her teeth sank through the gooey icing into the icy cake inside she had to put her hand over her mouth to keep from screaming with pain. Frozen Fig Newtons were child's play compared to this. Her teeth shivered down to the nerves with cold.

Suddenly she was aware of someone walking on the floor above her. Someone was walking across the kitchen. Maud looked toward the door at the top of the stairs. She had left it open! Her heart skipped a beat.

Lifting the cake with newfound energy, she ran to the fruit closet. She pulled a string dangling in front of her with her teeth. The lightbulb went on. Clutching the giant cake to her chest she scanned the many shelves for a hiding place.

The perfect container lay beneath the shelves on

the floor—a large, round hatbox. She knocked the top off with her foot and dropped the cake inside. It sounded as if she had dropped a cement block on the floor. The sound was louder than she had expected it would be. Her heart began racing as quickly as her thoughts.

What would happen when her mother discovered the cake was missing? She would be the immediate suspect. She was the only one who ever came downstairs besides her mother and the gasman. The gasman came down to check the meter in the basement at least once a month. He could have stolen it! Maybe he had a daughter named Lily, too, and her birthday was coming up and he didn't have any money to buy an extra-large chocolate cake with flowered icing. That sounded reasonable. Maud placed the lid over the hatbox and pushed it back against the wall.

I need an alibi, Maud thought. I'll say that John Henry was with me at the time of the crime. He'll back me up. She sighed with relief. It was an airtight case. The gasman did it.

Maud turned off the light and walked back to the freezer to collect the knife she had left on the floor. She took a look around to make sure she had covered her tracks. Everything seemed to be in order. She started up the steps. Just as she reached the kitchen and turned around to close the basement door, someone placed a hand on her shoulder.

"John Henry's mother just called," Mrs. Moser

said, tucking her hand back into her bathrobe pocket. She smelled like pine-scented bath salts.

"What about?" Maud asked, weak with relief.

"John Henry won't be able to walk to school with you on Monday. Apparently he had some sort of accident."

"An accident? What kind of accident?"

"I don't know any more about it than you do, Maudy. Mrs. Wilkes didn't offer any information and I didn't want to pry." She looked up at the clock above the stove. "Dinner should be ready by six." Mrs. Moser turned and walked out the door. The smell of pine lingered in the air where she had stood.

Maud leaned back against the kitchen wall, slid down to the floor and tried to sort out what her mother had just said. It didn't make sense. John Henry have an accident? Impossible. He was too young to have anything really bad happen to him. And what did Mrs. Wilkes mean when she said he wouldn't be able to walk to school with her on Monday? He was always there every morning, waiting outside the back door in the same old cowboy suit. She depended on him. The thought embarrassed Maud as though she had just admitted her affection out loud to her entire class at school.

"It's not that I really care about him," she silently explained to herself. "It's not as though he really means anything to me. I'm just used to him. The kid hasn't got a brain in his head. I even have to tell him to come in when it's cold outside."

She got up and went to the coat closet to get her jacket. "He probably just skinned his knee and is making a big deal out of it to get attention." She pulled on her jacket with one hand and yanked the front door open with the other.

"He's not getting any sympathy from me," she said in a firm voice. She was vaguely aware of her mother standing at the door yelling something about cucumbers as she broke into a run for the Wilkes' apartment.

15

Cowboy in Distress

It took Maud only three and a half minutes to get to John Henry's apartment building. They lived within a few city blocks of each other, but the climb up the narrow staircase seemed to take forever.

Maud leaned against the banister at the top of the stairs trying to catch her breath. The Wilkes lived in one of the oldest apartment buildings in the neighborhood. It didn't even have an elevator. It wasn't anything like the two-story brownstone house where her family lived.

She looked for the door with the small plastic Christmas wreath on it. Mrs. Wilkes must keep it on the door all year, Maud thought. The only other time she had visited John Henry's apartment was last summer. The Christmas wreath had been on the door then, too. The wreath was the only way Maud had of recognizing John Henry's apartment because most of the apartment numbers had been pulled off the doors by kids in the building.

The rug squished under her boots as she walked down the hallway. Maud remembered John Henry mentioning a water pipe that had broken in his building, but she had never imagined it would be like this. Water dripped down the walls. Nothing like that had ever happened at her house.

Maud spotted the wreath. She took off her jacket as she walked toward it. Her shirt was damp with sweat from running up the five flights of stairs. She knocked on the door and waited quietly. A long strip of wallpaper next to the Wilkes' apartment door was hanging down to the floor. It looked as though someone had ripped it on purpose.

She could hear the TV inside playing a rerun of a movie she had seen not long ago. The sound must have been turned up as far as it would go because she could hear every word the actors were saying. She knocked on the door again, more loudly this time. The tiny wreath fell off its nail to the floor. As Maud leaned down to pick it up the door opened.

A small woman wearing a large terry cloth bathrobe looked at her suspiciously through the half-opened door. Maud assumed that the woman standing in front of her must be Mrs. Wilkes. If she hadn't known that John Henry's mother had been a widow for almost as long as he had been alive she would have guessed that the bathrobe belonged to her husband. Her slender figure seemed lost inside it.

Mrs. Wilkes was a nurse. She worked the night shift at the local hospital. John Henry had often said that when his mother wasn't working, she was recuperating. She must be recuperating now, Maud thought.

"Who are you?" Mrs. Wilkes asked, her hand still

on the door as though she might slam it shut if she didn't like the answer.

"I'm Maudy . . . Maudy Moser . . . a friend of John Henry's."

"Oh!" she said and smiled with obvious delight. She opened the door and stepped to one side, making room for Maud to enter. "Come in, come in! I've heard so much about you."

Maud took two steps into the small entranceway and waited for further instructions. She wasn't sure what to expect. The one time she had been here before, Mrs. Wilkes had been away at the hospital.

"You know, I really am grateful to you, Maudy," Mrs. Wilkes said, as though they were old friends. She tightened the cord around her loose-fitting bathrobe and pushed up the sleeves that seemed to swallow her delicate hands and wrists. "For all the time my youngest spends over at your house after school I might have had to pay a babysitter, something I can't easily afford." Maud smiled politely and nodded.

"I love your hair," Mrs. Wilkes said, lightly touching Maud's head. Maud looked down at her shoes and blushed. There was an awkward silence.

"I like your bathrobe," Maud said, looking at a mustard stain on the bottom of her tattered robe.

"Relax, honey," Mrs. Wilkes said. She reached for a glass of amber-colored liquid on a small table by the door. "I'm just having a little something to quiet my nerves. Johnny gave me quite a scare today."

Maud had never heard John Henry called Johnny before. When he first introduced himself to her as John Henry, it had seemed to Maud that was what he liked to be called. She felt as though Mrs. Wilkes must be talking about someone else.

"What happened to him?" Maud asked softly.

Mrs. Wilkes motioned for her to wait in the entranceway as she disappeared into the living room. Maud heard children groaning and complaining as the TV sound was lowered. Mrs. Wilkes poked her head into the hall.

"Come on in the living room, honey."

The main room was a combination living room, dining room and den. Only one of the lamps was turned on. All of John Henry's brothers were lined up on the floor watching television.

"Boys," Mrs. Wilkes said, trying to get their attention. "I want you to meet Maudy . . . What did you say your last name was, honey?"

"Moser. M-O-S-E-R." She spelled out her last name. The only time she was ever asked her last name was on the first day of school each year when everyone was instructed to spell his name out so the teachers would be sure to write it correctly on their roll call sheets.

"Say hello to Maudy Moser, boys," Mrs. Wilkes said threateningly as she stood behind them. Two of the three boys glanced over their shoulders. The light from the TV illuminated their ruddy faces.

"Her hair changed colors," one of them said.

"I already met her last summer," the older boy said and went back to watching the movie. It was the same old stuff—cowboys and Indians clobbering each other in technicolor. The last time Maud had been here the boys had been watching a cowboy movie, too. No wonder John Henry is cowboy crazy, Maud thought.

Mrs. Wilkes smiled at Maud and shrugged her shoulders as if to say, "What can I do?" She walked to the linoleum-topped table in a corner of the room and sat down. She motioned for Maud to join her. Maud followed her to the dark corner and sat in a chair beside her.

Mrs. Wilkes leaned back and gazed contentedly at the TV as she sipped her drink. She didn't look so tired in the dim light.

For a moment she reminded Maud of a fragile porcelain doll Lily had given her one Christmas. That was the year Lily had spent all of her newspaper-route earnings on presents for everyone. She still remembered what a pretty face the doll had— big, brown glass eyes that opened and closed and a smiling mouth with little white teeth inside.

"What happened to him?" Maud asked quietly, not wanting to disturb anyone watching the movie.

"To Johnny?" Mrs. Wilkes asked, turning her head toward Maud. She was still watching the TV out of the corner of her eye. She looked as though she might be half-asleep.

"Yes," Maud said loudly. She was beginning to

think they had sold John Henry for the color set they seemed so intent on watching. One of the boys stretched out on the floor turned around and scolded her with a long, "Sh-h-h-h-h."

Just then a commercial flashed on the screen and all three boys jumped up and almost trampled each other in a mad rush for what Maud thought must be the kitchen.

As though suddenly awakened, Mrs. Wilkes put down her empty glass and sat up straight in her chair. "That was a nice movie," she said, stuffing a piece of dangling hair back into her ponytail. She held her wrist close to her face and looked at her watch. "Heavenly fathers," she gasped. "I have to get dressed or I'm gonna be late for work." She gave Maud's hand a quick pat and stood up. "You make yourself at home, honey. The fridge is in there." She pointed toward the room from which the boys were filing, holding sandwiches, cans of soda and bags of pretzels and potato chips clamped under their armpits. "Help yourself," she said and turned to walk away.

Maud jumped up and tapped her on the shoulder. "Wait," she said, embarrassed by her action but determined to find John Henry. "What happened to John Henry?" Mrs. Wilkes looked at her watch again and then told her.

"He got it into his head to go and baptize that cat you gave him in the bathtub today. The boys had to bring him to the hospital for stitches. Ten of them."

She held up both hands and spread her fingers as she said "ten."

Maud felt as though someone had given her heart a good hard squeeze. Today on the telephone she had told John Henry that animals had to be baptized if they wanted to go to heaven.

"If anyone in the apartment building so much as looks cross-eyed at that animal, it attacks them," Mrs. Wilkes said. "The next time I catch that nuisance I'm going to throw it out the window. I don't know why people don't declaw cats when they're born. Stitches aren't free, you know."

Maud nodded. "Can I see him?"

"I don't know where he is, but do me a favor and when you see him, flush him down the toilet."

"Not the kitten—John Henry. Can I see him?"

"Oh, sure. He's in the boys' room resting." She pointed to the closed door next to the kitchen. "Nice to meet you, Maudy," she said, taking Maud's limp hand in hers and giving it a quick shake. "I have to get dressed for work now." As soon as she left the room, Maud approached the closed door. She knocked twice, waited a short time and entered.

16

Angels for John Henry

"Maudy? Are you there, Maudy?"

"Yes, John Henry. I'm here."

Maud stood inside the closed door for a minute, waiting for her eyes to adjust to the darkness. A small night light soon made it apparent that the only pieces of furniture in the small room were two sets of bunk beds. Maud held one arm out protectively, like a blind girl exploring a new space, while she inched toward one of the bunk beds.

"Maudy? Maudy?"

The voice was coming from the other side of the room. She changed directions and crept forward.

"I'm coming, John Henry."

She sat down on the bottom bunk and gently patted the lump half hidden under the blanket.

"Maudy!" the voice screamed from above her. "Where are you?"

Maud leaned over the small form lying in the bed beside her and looked into the furry face of a life-size stuffed bear.

"Are you up there, John Henry?" she shouted toward the top bunk. In the darkness, she felt as though they were miles away from each other. There was no answer, but she heard something moving around on the mattress above.

"Come up here,'" John Henry's voice commanded as a slender beam of light shone down on the floor.

"Do you keep that flashlight in bed with you all the time?" she asked, putting her feet on the bottom rung of the ladder that led up to his bunk. There was no answer. When she reached the top, there was John Henry nodding his head. He held the flashlight directly on Maud's face, momentarily blinding her.

"Hey, cut it out," she said, taking the flashlight out of his hand.

"Your hair is funny," he said, squinching up his face.

"I dyed it," Maud said. "Like it?" John Henry nodded just as Maud knew he would. It wasn't hard to please John Henry Wilkes. She plopped down on the side of the bunk and dangled her legs over the edge. She waited for John Henry to say something, but all he did was breathe short deep breaths, each one making her feel guiltier. She turned off the flashlight and rolled it back and forth in her hands trying to think of something to say, some way to explain.

"Your mom told me what happened," she said, her back turned to him. She could feel him gently pulling at her shirttail.

"I baptized Snowball!" he said excitedly, as though he had just remembered the most important thing in his life. "She's gonna go to heaven." There was pride in his voice.

"That's good," she said slowly. She knew she had to say more than that. He had to be straightened out before he dumped every animal in the neighborhood into his mother's bathtub.

"You know what I was thinking, John Henry?" She could feel the bed moving slightly as he moved his head from side to side on the pillow. "I was thinking that maybe not all animals have to be baptized. You know, most animals are just naturally good and they go to heaven automatically."

"Uh-uh, he said quickly. "Snowball's mean. She had to get baptized."

"I don't think so, John Henry. I think she would have been O.K. even if you hadn't baptized her."

"But you told me," he said softly. His voice sounded strange. Maud turned around and looked at his dimly lit face. One of his small hands was covering half of it.

"Hey, cowboy, what are you hiding there?" she asked, gently removing his hand. She pointed the flashlight toward him and flipped the switch on. The instant the light hit his face she forgot everything that had happened that day. She forgot Lily and the secret baptism and the missing clothes—everything.

A long jagged cut sloped down John Henry's small, pale face from his eye to the middle of his cheek. It was a grownup cut on a child's face. She felt numb as she looked at the stitches caked with blood. She felt responsible for each thick black stitch. I might as well be a murderess, she thought. She could see that John Henry was concentrating hard on keeping the light out of his eyes. They were shut tight.

"Does it hurt?" she asked, surprised the words got past the lump in her throat. He nodded as two big tears squeezed past his tightly closed eyelids and rolled down the sides of his face into his ears. He covered the stitches with one hand.

"You told me!" he shouted angrily, pushing the flashlight out of his face. She obeyed his silent command and turned off the light.

"What?" she whispered. She wished she had never come.

"You said aminals have to be 'tized!" he cried, gulping down giant sobs between each word. Maud had never seen him this upset. He never got his words mixed up like other seven-year-olds. Every time his small body heaved she felt more and more frightened.

Suddenly Snowball appeared on the top bunk, silently stalking toward them on padded feet. She sat down next to John Henry's tear-streaked face and flicked his chin playfully with her tail. Maud watched the kitten scrape its small rough tongue across John Henry's forehead in an attempt to comfort him. John Henry looked up at Maud expectantly. At that moment Maud knew she had to say something.

"You're right, John Henry," she said, unsure of

what she would say next. She leaned over him, casting a shadow over his face. "I mean . . . I was right, animals do have to be baptized and it just so happens that I know for a fact that Snowball was the only animal left in the entire United States that needed baptizing." She held her breath, hoping he would believe her and fall asleep.

"How do you know?" he demanded as he caught his breath and punched her lightly on the arm.

"An angel told me last night." As the words came out of her mouth she watched John Henry's big blue eyes opening in complete acceptance and wonder.

"Angel?" he whispered and drew closer.

Maud knew that John Henry liked stories better than movies or even comic books—not the "once upon a time" kind, the "Maud" kind.

Snowball curled into a ball. She sucked the tip of her furry white tail as a baby might suck its bottle and purred contentedly.

"Well," Maud started, leaning back and closing her eyes for inspiration. "Last night I left my window open just a crack to get some fresh air and this beautiful woman in a long gown opened it up and flew inside."

She looked down at John Henry. He was lying back on the pillow running his fingers back and forth over his stitches. Maud pulled his hand away from his face.

"Billy and Ted say it's ugly, like Frankenstein," he said casually.

What horrible boys, Maud thought. I'm glad I have a sister instead of brothers.

"It's not ugly," she said. "In fact, it makes you look like you've just won a fight . . . like a real cowboy." John Henry's lips curled up at the corners as his eyes closed.

"Tell me more about the angel," he said dreamily.

"O.K. . . . Well, after she flew in the room, she sat down in my chair and read for a while until I woke up. She was too polite to wake me. All angels are very polite, you know." John Henry slowly nodded. "When I woke up she introduced herself as the Queen Angel and said I had been selected to come with her to a big shoot-out in the clouds that night because I had been so good and also because she had heard I liked to fly. So she stuck her hand in her pocket, and before I knew it she was sprinkling sparkly glittery little bits of angel dust all over me."

She felt John Henry's small warm hand slip inside her own. She squeezed it gently. It was hard not to like John Henry. He tried so hard. She looked down at him, waiting to be asked to continue with the story. His mouth dropped open slightly as he took long, deep, restful breaths. She tucked his hand under the blanket and sat listening to the TV blaring outside the door until she was sure he was asleep. She hoped his brothers wouldn't wake him when they came in to go to bed.

17

Eating the Evidence

Maud sat in her flying machine, knees drawn up to her chest, reading her favorite book, *Amelia Earhart: Portrait of a Flyer*. She turned the page and read out loud:

> "Amelia Earhart was only twenty-four years old when her parents and sister bought her a small, yellow Kinner Canary—her first plane."

Lucky Amelia, Maud thought. Her sister helped to buy her a plane. Lily won't even help me with my homework. She probably doesn't even know that I'm going to be a flyer. How could she know? She hasn't spoken to me since the baptism last week.

Maud leaned over and took a bite from the soggy mass of cake resting limply across her knees. She turned the page to a black-and-white photograph taken just before Amelia Earhart took her historic transatlantic flight in 1932. Maud closed her eyes and imagined herself in Amelia's place—the first woman to fly solo across the Atlantic Ocean. She could almost see the crowds of people gathering below as she circled over them in her plane—

"Here I am! I made it!" she would shout down to the insignificant looking specks that were her admirers on the ground below. Being an international celebrity and heroine did carry its responsibilities, so she decided to land her plane to shake the hand of the President. There was no time for signing autographs or making speeches. She had to get back up in the sky where she belonged. Quickly she dashed back into her plane and took off. "Let them eat cake," she shouted, throwing a giant cake attached to a parachute overboard. It floated down to the President, who immediately dug his finger in the icing and licked it off. "Chocolate," he shouted up to her. "It's my favorite flavor. Thanks, Maudy." She smiled down at him and waved as she flew off toward the horizon, her long scarf blowing in the wind behind her.

Maud scraped the last sweet remembrance of Lily's birthday cake from her knees and shook the crumbs from her sweater. It had taken almost one full week of sneaking down to the basement every day after school to finish off the cake. Now that it was finally eaten, she wished she had never seen it. As Lily's birthday dinner drew closer, she was beginning to realize her family would never believe the gasman was guilty.

In all the mystery books Maud had ever heard of the butler committed the crime, never the gasman. However, there was one major complication. The Mosers didn't have a butler. She was sure that she would be the most likely suspect. No one else in the family could have done it. Her mother was on a diet, her father was allergic to chocolate and grandmothers are never suspected of single-handedly eating their own granddaughter's birthday cake.

There was no turning back now. The cake was gone and tomorrow night was Lily's birthday dinner. The lump in Maud's stomach grew heavier.

Suddenly Maud heard the basement door opening.

"Maudy, are you down there?"

It was Lily's voice. Maud's heart raced like a murderer caught in the act. She held her breath, afraid that Lily might hear her breathing. The light turned on. She could hear Lily slowly coming down the stairs above her.

"Where are you? I know you're down here. I saw you go down."

She was trapped. She silently let the air out of her lungs, took another breath and held it. There was a chance that Lily might not find her under the staircase. She crossed all of her fingers.

"Why didn't you say something?" Lily said, appearing almost immediately from around the corner. Maud jumped up from her flying machine and quickly wiped her face clean with the sleeve of her sweater.

"Well, why didn't you?" Lily asked again. Maud shrugged her shoulders and waited to be accused of eating her cake.

"What do you do down here all the time?" Lily asked, picking up Maud's book.

"Read," Maud said softly as she turned a deep red. She felt angry at herself for blushing.

"What do you use for light? It's like a cave down here," Lily said. She shuddered as she looked at the spider webs hanging from the ceiling. Maud pointed to the flashlight at her feet and gave it a gentle kick. If only it had been a bomb, the whole thing would be over and she would never have to face tomorrow night.

"Is that your flying machine?" Lily asked with the beginning of a smile on her face. She looked like she was trying to keep from laughing.

Maud nodded as she looked down at the ground. She couldn't look Lily in the eyes. She knew how dumb she must look standing there inside what seemed to be an ordinary box. For the first time, Maud felt embarrassed by her flying machine. She wished it would disappear.

"Who told you about it?" Maud asked as she stepped out of the box.

"Mom."

The word hit her like a bullet. That's the last time I ever trust her with a secret, Maud thought.

"Hey," Lily said, putting her hand on Maud's shoulder. Maud looked up at her and smiled instinctively. "I made some cherry Jell-O. Want some?"

That was what Lily would probably be eating at her birthday dinner tomorrow night. Maud's face burned with guilt as she felt a burp squeezing up past her throat. She swallowed hard to force it back down. It made a funny noise halfway between her throat and her stomach.

"You sound hungry," Lily said, mistaking the noise. "Come on." She took Maud by the wrist and started to pull her toward the staircase. Maud followed slowly up the stairs behind her.

Maud tapped the Jell-O with her spoon and watched it jiggle before she took a bite.

"It's good," she said with her mouth still full. Lily nodded appreciatively. Maud noticed that she wasn't eating hers.

"Maudy, I've been calling the North Shore Baptist Church all week trying to find out what happened to our clothes, and the cleaning woman finally called back today. She said that she had picked them up by mistake in the dressing room. They're in the Lost and Found."

Lily was looking down at her Jell-O as though it were the most interesting sight in the world. Maud watched her quietly hack the shiny red gelatin to bits.

"I told you I didn't take them," Maud said, and then almost wished she hadn't. She felt sorry for Lily. She knew how hard it was to admit you were wrong.

"I know," Lily said looking up at her for an instant

and then down at her bowl of mutilated Jell-O. "I'm sorry about what happened, Maudy. I just didn't know who else to blame."

"I know," Maud said. All of the horrible things she had wanted to say disappeared. Lily pushed back her dish, untouched.

"Anyway . . . Claire and I are going ice skating tonight at Brown Deer Park. Do you want to come?"

Maud tried desperately to keep herself from appearing overly pleased, but it was impossible. She looked up at Lily and smiled with delight.

"Good," Lily said, taking Maud's expression as a definite "yes." She got up and started out the door. "Claire's coming over at seven."

"O.K.," Maud said. She was so excited about tonight that she helped herself to another bowl of cherry Jell-O.

"What's wrong, Maudy?" Grand asked at dinner. "You're quieter than usual."

Nothing was wrong. She was thinking about how tonight was going to be different. This time she wasn't going to embarrass Lily by being her younger tag-along sister. She was going to fit in if it killed her.

Right after dinner Maud went directly to her parents' bathroom and locked herself inside. She sat down at her mother's dressing table and surveyed the cosmetics scattered on top. If she carried out her plan she would have to sneak by her parents on her way out of the house. This was the first time she could remember their staying in on their usual Evening Out. She was certain that they wouldn't appreciate her new image.

Dipping her fingers into a jar of pink cream, she slowly smeared it over her cheeks. Next came mascara and then eye shadow. Selecting eye shadow was difficult. There were so many colors. Finally, she chose blue to go with her eyes and white to match her skates. A little lipstick and she'd be ready to go. Someone knocked on the bathroom door.

"Maudy, are you in there?" It was Lily.

"Yeah," she said, opening her mother's drawer full of lipsticks.

"I've been looking for you everywhere. Claire is here. Are you ready?"

"In a minute."

"What are you doing?"

She didn't want to tell. It had to be a surprise.

"I'm taking a bath," she said, thinking of her mother and giggling.

"Claire and I don't want to wait around, so just meet us at the north end of the skating rink. O.K.?"

"O.K.," Maud said as she found an entire box full of different colored lipsticks. One of them was labeled "Cherry." That's the one for me, Maud thought. She looked at herself in the mirror. Lily was right. Makeup did make a difference. She was sure she looked at least twelve and a half.

After getting her ice skates and ankle supports Maud stood at the top of the stairs to see if the coast was clear. Grand had left for the theatre earlier and her parents were in the living room. She couldn't wait any longer. The skating rink was only a block and a half away, but she was already late. She had to risk walking by her parents on her way out. Maud carefully wound her scarf around her newly painted face, flung the end back over her shoulder and raced down the stairs for the front door.

"Maudy, don't you want to sit by the fire with us for a while?" her mother asked from the living room.

"No thanks, Mom," Maud answered in a muffled voice through her scarf. She turned the doorknob. "I'm going skating."

She left in such a hurry that she forgot to close the door behind her.

18

Lily Comes to the Rescue

No one ever used the warm-up house at Brown Deer Park's skating rink. It smelled like dirty socks and dog urine, and all of the candy machines inside were busted.

Some people put on their skates in their cars. The ones who were lucky enough to live close to the park walked and changed into their skates on one of the wooden benches surrounding the rink.

By the time Maud arrived the benches were already covered with boots. She pushed them aside to make room for herself and sat down. She pulled her foam rubber ankle supports out of her jacket pockets, and inserted them into her skates. Maybe these will make the difference, she thought.

Maud was tired of being the ugly duckling on ice, ankles caved in, skating on the inside leather of her skates rather than on the blades. Holding the ankle supports in place, she carefully slipped her feet inside. She had to take off her thick wool mittens to get a better grip on the laces. Her hands worked quickly to tie a bow before they turned numb from the bitter cold.

She wished she could check her makeup, but she had forgotten to bring along a mirror. She sat for a moment watching the activity on the ice. Skating rinks were special places—like theatres—only here there was no audience. Everyone was on stage.

Maud kept her eyes down on the ice as she tested her balance. She knew that looking up into one of the large, white floodlights surrounding the rink would be disastrous. It was like looking into the sun. Once last winter, fascinated by the floodlight's over-powering brilliance, she had stared at it for several seconds. She hadn't been able to skate most of that night because of the colored dots that seemed to dance in front of her eyes.

She half-walked, half-skated forward in short, jerky steps. She had hoped her ankles would be stronger this year, but they collapsed inward and dragged along the ice just as they had done last winter. Even her new ankle supports didn't help. They just made her ankles look fat.

Last year, with a lot of practice, she had managed to adapt to skating on her ankles rather than on her skate blades. By swinging her arms she had found that she could move a little faster. Remembering, she waved her arms around and glided forward. Her ankles ached from the effort.

She noticed a line of kids from Lily's class racing toward her at full speed. Maud nearly toppled over trying to get out of their way, but they managed to stop short of her.

"Hi," Maud said, looking at all the new faces sizing

her up. She recognized only two of them—Lily and Claire. Lily was looking at her with a worried expression on her face.

"Hi," Lily said. She turned away before Maud could answer. "Come on," Lily cried, trying to get the group's attention. "Let's see who can make it to the other side of the rink the fastest." No one moved.

"Hey, who's the clown?" one of the boys in front asked. Although he was looking straight at Maud she didn't know who he was talking about. She looked around the rink.

"Where?" Maud asked. Everyone laughed, but they seemed to be laughing much too long. Claire was whispering something in the boy's ear. Maud couldn't hear what she was saying, but a broad grin was spreading across his face. Lily was still trying to get the group interested in racing to the other side of the rink.

"Word has it that she's Lily's little sister," the boy standing next to Claire announced. Everyone looked at Lily this time and laughed loudly. Lily looked angry or embarrassed, Maud couldn't tell which.

One of the boys turned to Lily. "Stuck babysitting little Miss America, huh, Lily?" he said. Lily nodded and looked up into a floodlight. Maud wanted to warn her not to do it, but she couldn't say anything in front of all those kids. "Does that mean you're not going out for pizza with us later?" he asked.

"Of course I'm going," Lily said, blinking her eyes as she turned away from the floodlight.

Most of the kids had lost interest in Maud and were skating off. Maud could hardly believe what she saw. Some of them were holding hands and skating in pairs around the rink as if they were grownups. Just last winter, the boys in Lily's class had been interested only in playing ice hockey by themselves. As soon as everyone else left, Lily and Claire scrutinized her face as though they were seeing it for the first time.

"Randy was right," Claire said, giggling. "She does sort of look like a clown."

"Why are you wearing all that goop on your face?" Lily asked angrily.

Suddenly Maud realized who the clown was. She hid her face behind her mittens. It was as though one of the giant floodlights had come crashing down on her head. If only it had. Then she would be dead and no one would have laughed at her.

"I can wear makeup if I want to," Maud mumbled. She looked at the pink cream that had come off on the palms of her mittens. She didn't feel twelve and a half anymore. She didn't even feel eleven.

"Oh, Maudy," Lily sighed. "You put way too much on. You're too young to be fooling around with makeup. You're just a child."

"And what are you?" Maud demanded.

"Well, for one thing, I'm a lot older than you are."

"That's for sure," Claire murmured in agreement. Lily looked at Claire out of the corner of her eye and smiled appreciatively.

"You're only two years older than me," Maud said defiantly.

"Than I," Lily corrected, looking down at Maud's swollen ankles. "Are your ankle supports helping, Maudy?" she asked.

"Don't try and change the subject," Maud said. "You're only two years older."

Lily looked up into a floodlight over Maud's head. This time Maud didn't have the slightest urge to stop her.

"Do you want to know the difference between you and me?" she asked. Maud didn't see any point in saying no. Lily was going to tell her anyway.

"I am a woman," she said slowly. She looked at Claire who quickly nodded in agreement. With renewed confidence, Lily looked back at Maud and repeated in a calm voice. "I am a woman. You are a child. Children do not wear makeup."

"You are not," Maud blurted. "You're a girl, just like me."

"I'm menstruating," Lily said as if that settled the issue.

"We could have babies if we wanted to," Claire added coolly. Maud had a sudden urge to shove them both into a snowbank.

"Hey, Lily! Claire!" a girl shouted as she skated past. "We're having another race on the other side of the rink." The girl was heading for a group of boys standing in front of the warm-up house.

Without a word, Lily and Claire took off at full

speed behind the girl. "Wait up!" they shouted. "We're coming!" Maud watched them skate away, knowing that she'd never be able to keep up.

She propelled herself to the nearest snowbank and collapsed. Scooping up a handful of snow, she took a bite. It made her teeth ache. She took another bite anyway, closed her eyes as if to make a wish and rubbed the remains over her face. It burned. The wind felt like hundreds of needles flying into her wet face. She could almost taste the bitter cold through her skin.

She felt the years sliding away on the palms of her mittens as she wiped the makeup off her face. She was eleven again. But it didn't matter anymore. With or without eye shadow, she would never fit in with Lily's friends.

Maud thought back to the first night Lily came home from camp and moved out of their room. It had all started then. What had she done to make Lily want to leave her? Maybe Lily got tired of her. Maud feared that she was boring.

She kicked her legs out and looked at her swollen ankles. I look as if I just had an unsuccessful ankle transplant, she thought unhappily. No wonder Lily is embarrassed to be seen with me. I'm a mess—a boring, dull mess.

Just then a small girl flew past. She spun around twice, leaped into the air and came down skating backwards. Maud envied her strong, straight ankles and effortless style.

She decided to get out on the ice one last time

before going home. This will be my farewell skate, Maud thought, slowly hoisting herself up. She pushed away from the snowbank, determined to stand on her own two blades. She managed to balance on them for a few seconds and felt as though she were silently gliding through the air on a motorless plane. Then her ankles caved in and her moment of flight was over. She went back to sliding around on the insides of her ankles.

She scratched out a star on the ice with the tip of her skate, then added a stem to transform the star into a flower. She wanted to show it to Lily, but she was at the other end of the rink with her friends. They looked like they were going to have a race. Maud scraped her skate through the flower.

Nothing was the same without Lily. Half the reason Maud liked doing things was because she looked forward to going home and telling Lily about them. Life without Lily was a terrible thing.

Maud began skating in small circles around the crossed out flower. She dragged one skate behind herself to etch the circles in ice. She looked across the rink again. All the kids were spread out in a long line, crouched over, waiting for the race to begin. She went back to making circles, concentrating on making the smallest and most perfect circle possible. The voices from across the rink were distracting her. She tried to ignore them and listen to the music coming from the loudspeaker, but the voices kept getting louder and louder.

She was almost managing to enjoy herself when

someone yelled "Watch out!" An elbow hit her face and the next thing she knew, she was flying across the ice on her stomach.

Maud lay on the ice with her eyes closed. The sound of skates sliding and scraping across the rink competed with the blaring old-time music.

"Why didn't you get out of the way?"

Maud opened her eyes. A dozen faces were looking down at her as though she were a new animal at the zoo. Some were giggling and whispering. Others looked concerned. A boy standing near her feet repeated his question.

"I'm sorry. I couldn't stop in time. Why didn't you get out of the way?"

All of the faces turned to look at him. Claire skated up beside the boy and started yelling. Maud was too stunned to move, so she just lay there, watching.

"Randy, did you skate into her?" Claire demanded.

"It's not my fault," Randy shouted back. "How was I supposed to know she'd get in the middle of the race? I yelled out at her. She just stood there like a goon."

"You're the goon, Randy Taylor," said an angry voice. Someone was pushing through the crowd. It was Lily. She fell to her knees on the ice and cradled Maud's head in her lap.

"Are you O.K.?" she asked frantically. She pulled

off one of her mittens and held it gingerly under Maud's nose. Maud flinched from the slight pressure.

"Does that hurt, Maudy?" Lily asked in an alarmed voice. Maud nodded and looked up into Lily's fair windburned face. For a moment Maud forgot her own discomfort. She wasn't aware of anything but the tears running down Lily's cheeks.

Lily began gently squeezing Maud's arms and legs, checking for broken bones. Maud lay limp as a rag doll, watching Lily take over. Most of the kids skated away. Only Claire and Randy remained.

"Are you all right?" Lily asked. She rocked Maud back and forth. The mitten dropped from Maud's nose. It was saturated with blood. Maud hadn't realized she was bleeding that much, but she wasn't frightened. As long as Lily's arms were around her, nothing else seemed to matter.

"Ooooooooh, look," Claire said, pointing to the bloody mitten.

"Don't look at me," Randy said defensively as he shrugged his shoulders.

"I wasn't looking at you," Claire said in a disgusted voice. "I was looking at that mitten. Look at it. She could be hemorrhaging or something." Lily gave Claire a threatening look.

"Don't listen to her, Maudy. She doesn't know what she's talking about. Everything's going to be all right," Lily said reassuringly.

"It wasn't my fault," Randy said, sticking his hands deep into his pockets as he shifted uncomfortably from skate to skate. "You're O.K., aren't you?" he asked Maud. She slowly nodded. "Looks to me like you just have a bloody nose."

"What do you know?" Lily snapped.

"She's O.K.," he said and skated off.

Lily pulled off her other mitten and threw it toward Claire.

"Fill it with snow," she said. Claire quickly packed the mitten with snow and handed it back to Lily. She pressed the cold wet mitten against the side of Maud's nose.

"This will stop the bleeding, Maudy. Just lie back and relax." Every muscle in Maud's body seemed to melt as she let her weight rest against Lily.

"I think Randy was right, Lily," Claire said, looking toward the kids at the other end of the rink. "It's probably just a bloody nose."

"You don't know that for sure," Lily said. "And I'm not taking any chances." Claire looked surprised.

"All right, all right, big sister. Calm down. Don't you think you're overreacting a little?"

"Look Claire, if you want to skate with the others, then go."

"Aren't you coming? Everybody's going to that new pizza place on Grant Street. Maudy can get home by herself. Can't you, Maudy?"

"Yeah," Maud said softly. "I guess so." She didn't want Lily to leave her so she groaned a little.

"What is it, Maudy?" Lily asked. "You're in pain, aren't you?"

"No," Maud said as painfully as possible.

"Help me get her home," Lily said. "We can meet everyone later."

Claire didn't look overjoyed by Lily's suggestion. She dug her skates in the ice and looked over at the kids by the warm-up house. They were getting ready to leave the rink.

"Come on, Lily," Claire said. "She'll be all right. She said so herself. You can see that it's only a bloody nose. Come on . . ."

"Leave," Lily shouted. "I'm staying."

"O.K.," Claire said, turning around. "Suit yourself. See you later." Claire waved one arm behind her as she skated off.

"I hope you puke on your pizza," Lily said under her breath.

Maud flinched to see if Lily regretted her decision to stay. Lily immediately held her tighter.

"Don't worry, Maudy," Lily said. "I'm here. I won't leave you. Everything will be fine once we're home." She planted three kisses on her forehead. Maud counted them. She didn't want to forget tonight, not any of it.

Lily helped her stand up, even though she didn't really need any help, and they walked to the bench together to take off their skates.

Maud limped all the way home to make sure Lily kept her arm hooked around hers, the way she sometimes walked with Claire. Maud had never been happier in the entire eleven years of her life.

19

The Magnificent Moser Sisters

Maud felt warm and lazy as she lay gazing dreamily at a smudge on her bedroom ceiling. She had gone back to sleeping on the upper bunk last week after the disastrous baptism ceremony. Being in a high place always helped lift her spirits. She moistened her finger on her tongue, reached up and extended the smudge on the ceiling.

Michelangelo must have started this way, she thought. Mrs. Obemeyer had told her class about the famous Italian artist who painted the entire ceiling of a chapel lying on his back. Maud was sorry she hadn't asked Mrs. Obemeyer what color Michelangelo had painted it. She would have liked to know. She looked up at her picture. A smudge or two more and it would be completed—a flying auto named the Aerocar, her current favorite.

Pulling the thick down comforter over her head, Maud squirmed happily under the covers. Her feet had felt like two frozen meatloaves on the way home tonight. Now, safely tucked inside her magic fur boots, they felt warm and comfortable.

She removed the ice pack her mother had fixed

for her and sat up. Her nose had stopped bleeding. Just to make sure that it was back in good working order, she closed her mouth and inhaled deeply. The faint sweet scent of lilacs rushed up her nostrils. It was the pleasingly familiar smell of Lily's talcum powder. Lily used it after every shower and as a result all of her clothes smelled like lilacs. Maud giggled, suddenly delighted with the idea of a girl named Lily smelling like lilacs.

She was glad that she had lied to Lily about her pajamas being in the wash. Otherwise, she might never have gotten the opportunity to borrow Lily's new flannel nightgown. She gave herself a hug. Wearing something of Lily's made her feel divinely special. She wished Claire could be here to see her now. She would never believe Lily had let her wear one of the matching nightgowns unless she saw it for herself.

She slid back under the covers. What did she care what Claire thought? She placed the ice pack against the bruise on her cheek and kicked the neatly tucked sheets out from the bottom of her bed. She wasn't a bit sleepy and there was nothing to do, so she started tapping out songs on her two front teeth with her fingernail. She was tapping out the theme song to a toothpaste commercial when the bedroom door opened. Lily entered, carrying a china pitcher in one hand and a plate piled high with toast and a single Fig Newton balancing on top. A book was tucked under one arm.

"Claire just called from the new pizza place on Grant Street," Lily said.

"So what?" Maud grumbled.

"She says it's great. I'm meeting her there in a little while so I won't be able to stay here with you much longer."

That was the last straw! Here she was on her deathbed and Lily was going off with that creep. She was tired of sharing Lily. Enough was enough. Tonight was hers. She wouldn't let Lily leave her. She would charm her into staying.

With one sweep of her hand Lily knocked all the papers and books off Maud's desk top and set down the pitcher and plate of toast. She poured the piping hot chocolate into two ceramic mugs, handed Maud one of them with the Fig Newton and disappeared into the lower bunk with the entire plate of toast. After Maud had eaten her precious cookie, a hand holding a single slice of buttered cinnamon toast suddenly appeared by the side of Maud's mattress. "Thanks," Maud said and grabbed it before Lily could change her mind.

"I'm going to read to you," Lily said in a garbled voice. Maud could tell she was talking with her mouth full. "O.K.," Maud said. It was wonderful talking to Lily like this, bunk to bunk, like the good old days. "You have a nice clear reading voice," Maud added sweetly. She wondered if she should compliment Lily on the amount of cinnamon she put on the toast now or wait a while.

"You never told me that before," Lily said.

Maud's memory flashed back to when Lily had shared this room with her and the many fights they had had. Could it be that she hadn't appreciated Lily until she left her? Distance does make the heart grow fonder, Maud mused as she sucked the cinnamon off her fingers. Maybe the good old days really weren't so good.

Maud could hear Lily flipping through the pages of a book. She took a sip of hot chocolate while she waited for Lily to find an interesting page. It burned the roof of her mouth. She would have preferred a nice cold glass of iced tea, but she didn't say anything.

She propped the mug up on her pillow and opened the ice pack. She fished around inside for a small ice cube and held it at arm's length above the mug. When she let it drop, chocolate-brown spots appeared all around the mug on her pillow case. The ice cube was diminishing rapidly in her hot chocolate.

"Here's something," Lily said suddenly. She cleared her throat and began reading out loud:

"Lost in an endless blur of fog and cloud, they flew toward what they hoped was the English coast. They began climbing the 4,000-foot altitude to surmount the overcast. The clouds resembled icebergs in the distance."

Maud nearly choked on her toast. That was one of her favorite passages from her book, the one she had left in her flying machine.

"Is that my book?" Maud interrupted.

"Yes. You don't mind, do you?"

"No," Maud lied. If Lily noticed what she had written on the inside of the cover, she would die of embarrassment. Lily would be sure to laugh.

"Here," Lily said. "This part is much better." With relief, Maud realized Lily must have been too busy skipping around to what she often referred to as the "juicy parts" to bother with the inside of the cover. She gulped down her cooled chocolate as Lily began reading:

"George Palmer Putnam proposed to Amelia in a hangar at an aircraft factory while she was waiting for her plane to be warmed up. To his surprise, she nodded in agreement and ran off to climb into the cockpit of her plane. Putnam was stunned. He could hardly believe that she had accepted. He had proposed to her six other times. But Amelia Earhart always made up her mind on the spur of the moment and then stuck by her decision . . .

"Wow," Lily said. "That's how I'm going to live my life."

"How?" Maud asked yawning. This was the only part of the book that bored her.

"By the spur of the moment. That's how I'm going to live my life. As soon as I turn eighteen, I'm leaving home and becoming an artist."

"What kind?" Maud asked. Lily had been talking

about what she was going to do when she turned eighteen for as long as Maud could remember.

"An actress or a painter . . . probably an actress. I've already been in two school plays. And besides, acting is in the Moser blood. Look at Grand."

Maud wondered if flying might be in the Moser blood, too. She knew she could feel it in her bones, but she wasn't too sure about her blood.

"There's just one problem," Lily continued.

"What?" Maud asked dutifully.

"I'm definitely going to have to dye my eyebrows if I'm an actress."

"Why?" Next to Lily's long feet Maud thought Lily's best feature was her barely visible yellow-white eyebrows.

"Mrs. Seaman says that an audience reads the actor's character by her vocal and facial expression." Mrs. Seaman was the upper school's drama coach. She had thick woolly eyebrows and a black mustache. "How can the audience see the expression on my face under bright stage lights when I look like an old faded dish towel."

Here it comes, Maud thought, shifting into a more comfortable position. It always starts this way. First, Lily calls herself a faded dish towel and then . . .

"How many actresses do you know who are as pale as I am? None," Lily said before Maud had a chance to respond. "Harry Jensen said that the pale yellow streaks in my hair look as if someone cracked an egg over my head. Did I tell you that? Did I?"

Maud nodded, even though she knew Lily

couldn't see her. There was no point in answering. Lily was picking up speed now.

"I felt like a freak for ages after that . . . And then of course there are my almost invisible eyebrows." She always said "invisible eyebrows" the loudest, because she hated them the most.

"I can see your eyebrows," Maud said.

"Well, you're the only one who can. Mother won't let me dye my eyebrows like she let you dye your hair," she said bitterly.

"Mom didn't *let* me dye my hair, Lily. Honest." Maud nearly fell off her bed trying to explain. "I did it on my own. Mom got really mad, but if you want to have dark eyebrows that much you should just go ahead and dye them without asking like I did."

"I can't. Mother hid the dye. I already checked. Besides, I don't want to use that kid stuff. Vegetable dye rinses out. I need the permanent kind. I mean business, Maudy."

"I know," Maud said sadly. She hadn't known that Lily thought her mother let her dye her hair.

"I probably won't get any parts in plays when I'm in high school because of my overall paleness. Mother is ruining my life. Anyway, I'm going to leave home and dye them as soon as I turn eighteen. How is the audience ever going to know if my character is happy or sad if they can't see my eyebrows?"

"Because if you're happy, you'll be smiling," Maud said thoughtfully. "And if you're not happy, you won't be."

"Smiles aren't enough," Lily said. "I'm leaving home."

Maud leaned back on her pillow and sighed. Lily was probably right. She lifted the ice pack from her bruised nose. It wasn't helping anymore. She didn't like thinking about Lily leaving home. It made her feel emptier than the inside of a doughnut.

"Lily?"

"Yeah."

"Will you take me with you when you leave home?"

"I can't, Maudy. When I'm eighteen, you'll be only sixteen and that's too young to live on the spur of the moment."

Maud felt like crying. She couldn't tell which was bothering her more, the constant dull ache in her cheek or what Lily was saying.

"But when I'm ninety, you'll be ninety-two," Maud said. "Both of us will be old. We'll have been sisters a long time then." She suspected that Lily was reading to herself because she didn't answer for a moment.

"Yeah," Lily said. "Maybe I'll take you along."

Maud went over the words in her head. Maybe I'll take you along, maybe I'll take you along, until the "maybe" disappeared altogether. I will take you along. She was sure that was what Lily had said.

"Wow," Lily cried suddenly. "It says here that Amelia Earhart wore a brown suit at her wedding."

Maud slipped the empty mug under her pillow.

Sometimes Lily got excited about the oddest things. Maud watched Lily as she climbed up the ladder to her bunk, balancing the plate of toast on her book. Maud quickly curled up her legs to make more room for Lily. If she was comfortable she might decide to stay.

"Lean back and your nose will stop bleeding," Lily instructed. Maud didn't say it had already stopped.

Lily leaned against the wall and propped the book up against her knees. The two of them ate in silence, Lily paging through the book while Maud counted the pretty drops of dried blood on her pillow. After the last piece of cinnamon toast had been eaten, Lily yawned and stretched out, her head at the opposite end of the bed, her feet next to Maud. She opened the book above her head and started reading out loud:

"Aviation became almost an obsession with Amelia Earhart after her father took her to an air show at Long Beach."

"What does obsession mean?" Maud asked.

"It means she could hardly think of anything except flying, she loved it so much."

"Oh," Maud said almost in a whisper. "That's how it is with me."

Lily raised her head a little and looked at Maud. She dropped her head back down again and continued reading:

"A short time later Amelia discovered how much it cost to learn to fly: one thousand dollars. She took a job at the Los Angeles telephone company to take care of the expense and immediately signed up for flying lessons."

"How much do you think it would cost to learn to fly now?" Maud asked softly.

Lily raised herself on one elbow and looked steadily into Maud's eyes. Maud turned red with embarrassment.

"What did you say?" Lily asked.

"Nothing," Maud said, lying back on the pillow. "Go on." Lily collapsed once again and continued reading:

"From then on Amelia worked all week to pay for her flying lessons and spent the weekends at a dusty airfield a few miles from town. The exhilaration of soaring into the sky was so great that she could hardly bear coming back to earth."

Lily sat up and looked at Maud. "Why did you say that about flying lessons?"

Maud crawled down under her covers. She felt more protected there. "I don't know," she said, watching Lily's face carefully for any sign of disbelief.

Lily began paging through the book. Maud froze

when she saw Lily stop at the inside of the front cover. She had seen it. PILOT MOSER. Why hadn't she erased it before? Lily would never stop teasing her. Maud shut her eyes and burrowed further under the covers. Lily would tell Claire and they'd laugh. The whole school would find out and she'd have to leave town. She would run away tomorrow. She would take the money she had been saving for flying lessons and run away . . .

It was hot under the covers. She felt as if she were smothering, but she couldn't come up for air, not with Lily there. She would never be able to face her again.

Maybe if I'm quiet enough, she'll think I'm asleep, Maud thought. She'll think I'm asleep and she'll leave. Maybe she'll forget she ever saw it.

She felt Lily moving around on the bed. Good, Maud thought, she's getting ready to leave. Just as she began to relax, she felt a cool rush of air as the covers lifted off her. Lily was lying next to her.

"You really want to be one, don't you?" Lily asked. Maud shrugged her shoulders. "You know, I think you'd make a really good flyer," Lily said casually. Maud turned around and looked at Lily. She wasn't even grinning.

"Like Amelia Earhart?" Maud whispered. Lily nodded.

"I think you could be just about anything you wanted to be, Maudy. You mess up a lot, but you try harder than anyone I know. Sometimes I wish I could be a little more like you."

Maud smiled so hard her face felt as if it might crack in half. Lily was looking at a strand of her hair as though she were checking for split ends, but Maud knew she was embarrassed by what she had said.

"When I'm a pilot I'll fly you to theatres all over the world," Maud said, watching Lily's face break into a smile. Lily rolled over on her back and stuffed Maud's pillow under her head. Maud snuggled close to her.

"You'll be a famous flyer and I'll be a famous actress. They'll call us The Magnificent Moser Sisters," Lily said with the dramatic flair only a real actress can show. "You'd better start saving your money for those flying lessons." Lily closed her eyes. There was a faint smile on her face, a lovely pale smile.

Maud watched her for a minute and then lay back and closed her own eyes. She wanted to say that she had been saving money for flying lessons for months, but she didn't want to disturb Lily. Actresses need their rest. Lily would probably say that getting enough rest was almost as important as having dark, expressive eyebrows.

All of the tension in Maud's body seemed to melt away. She felt cool and light as though the enormous weight she had been carrying around these past few months had suddenly been lifted. She always knew she had been meant to fly. But she needed someone else, just one other person to know it, too. So she, Maud Moser, would be a flyer. Lily had said so, and she knew what she was talking about.

As Maud was curling up into a ball, getting situated for the night, Lily sat up and groaned loudly.

"Oh, no! It's almost nine-thirty," Lily said, looking anxiously at her wristwatch. "I was supposed to meet Claire at nine." Maud had hoped she would spend the night in the bunk bed for old time's sake. Her wish dissolved as she watched Lily scrambling down the ladder. She had to act fast or she'd lose Lily for the evening.

Maud gently bumped her nose against the mattress. She lifted her head and looked at the sheet. No blood. She stuck two fingers up her nostrils and pulled them out. Still, nothing. She blew through her nose as hard as she could. A light spattering of blood fell on her white pillow case.

"Lily!" Maud shouted happily. Lily looked up as she was pulling on one of her boots. "My nose is bleeding again," Maud said, pointing to the drops of blood on her pillow case.

"Lean back like I told you and it'll stop," Lily said, pulling on the other boot.

"It's gushing down the back of my throat. I think I'm going to choke to death," Maud insisted, taking her throat in both hands in a dramatic gesture.

"I'll tell Mom to come up before I leave," Lily said. She was heading for the door.

"Lily?" Lily turned to face her, nervously tapping her foot on the floor.

"Yes. What is it?"

"All the ice in my ice pack is melted," Maud

dangled the limp ice pack over the side of the bed.

"You'll have to go down to the kitchen and get some more ice yourself, Maudy. I don't have the time." She started out the door again.

"Lily!" Maud screamed. Lily's leg stopped in midair. She turned around with an annoyed look on her face. "What is it? I have to go," she said in a final tone of voice. When Maud looked at Lily's face she knew she couldn't stall any longer.

"Lily . . . do you like me as much as Claire?" She shielded herself with a pillow and timidly looked over the top of her headboard. Lily sighed and looked up at the ceiling. Suddenly, she looked very tired.

"Maudy, don't you know?" Maud shook her head. "Claire and I are just friends. We're sisters. Nothing can change that." Lily glanced down at her wristwatch and rushed out the door.

Lily had said, "We're sisters" as though it were something bigger, better than friendship. Maud stared at the empty doorway for a long time and then she sat up in bed and dangled her legs over the edge. Lily was right. They would always be sisters. Nobody could ever change it, no matter how hard they tried. Not even Claire. The knowledge swept over Maud like a giant wave. The overpowering emptiness she had felt since Lily had returned from summer camp dwindled to the size of her baby finger.

She grabbed the ice pack, jumped off her bed and

descended the staircase, landing on every other step. She bumped into her mother as she raced into the kitchen.

"How are you feeling?" her mother asked, taking Maud's face into her hands and checking her color.

"Better," Maud said, shaking free and heading for the refrigerator.

"What do you want out of there?" Mrs. Moser asked. "From the looks of things you and Lily have eaten quite enough this evening." She nodded toward the empty package of Fig Newtons and an open loaf of bread lying on the counter. Maud remembered what Lily had once told her. People are either cooks or cleaner-uppers, not both.

"I need ice," she said, holding up the ice pack. "It's all melted."

"I don't think you'll need that anymore tonight," her mother said, taking the ice pack from her hand. She gently pushed Maud toward the door. "Now get back in bed and try to get some sleep. I don't want you starting another nose bleed tonight."

Maud walked out the kitchen door. As soon as she was out of her mother's sight, she started twirling around in Lily's nightgown. When she began to get dizzy she stopped and headed for the stairs. Lily was getting her jacket from the coat closet. Maud sat down on the bottom step and silently watched her.

"What kind of pizza are you going to get?" she asked. Lily turned around.

"Why aren't you back in bed?" Maud shrugged

her shoulders. "I don't know what kind I'm going to get." Lily pulled a wrinkled dollar bill and some odd change out of her jeans pocket. "Probably the cheapest."

"Have a nice time," Maud said as Lily opened the front door.

"Don't forget my birthday dinner tomorrow, Maudy," Lily said over her shoulder. "We're going to have an incredible cake. I helped Mom pick it out." The door slammed shut behind her.

Maud stood up and slowly walked to the door. As she opened it a gust of wind puffed out Lily's nightgown and swirled her hair all around her head. She looked up at the sky. The stars were out. It would be a clear day tomorrow—a pilot's dream.

She cupped both her hands around her mouth to make a sort of megaphone.

"Hey, Lily!" she shouted.

"Yeah," she heard in the distance. "What is it?"

"About the cake . . ."

"What?" Lily's voice drifted back faintly.

"Never mind," Maud said. "I'll tell you about it to-morrow."

She slammed the door shut and twirled around in Lily's nightgown one more time before starting up to bed.

20

A Matter of Life and Death

Just as Maud was beginning to drop off to sleep her body tensed and she sat up in bed.

"I must be crazy," she whispered to the tree swaying in the wind outside her window. "I can't tell Lily that I ate her whole birthday cake." She cuddled up with Boris the boa constrictor and tried to explain to him. "Lily's basically a good person and I know that she loves me, but when she finds out that I've eaten her birthday cake, she'll kill me."

After all, sisterly love could only stretch so far. Maud knew that if Lily ever ate her birthday cake, she'd feel the same way. She wrapped Boris's long velvet body around her shoulders and jumped down from the top bunk. She paced back and forth along the line of stuffed animals propped against the wall.

"I need help. I can't do this alone," she told them. Sixteen pairs of button eyes glared back at her. She swatted each one of them with Boris's soft velvet tail and walked over to the window.

The weather had changed quite suddenly. It had turned into a blustery night, so windy that Maud wondered how the stars managed to keep themselves from blowing across the sky.

"Maybe Lily will get food poisoning at the new pizza place tonight and the birthday dinner will be postponed," she whispered to the tree. One of its long, thin branches stretched out and tapped against the windowpane as if to scold her. She was immediately sorry for having such a thought. Wishing for someone to get sick was a terrible thing to do, especially if it was your own sister. Besides, the chances were one in a thousand that she would get food poisoning anyway.

Maud wound Boris around her waist twice and tied his long, green face and tail into a knot. She opened the window. The dry icy air raced inside, penetrating her thin flannel nightgown and chilling her to the bone. Her first impulse was to close the window and climb back into her warm bed, but she didn't. Instead, she just stood there, a whipping post for the wind. Goose bumps rippled over her arms and legs. Her nose ached from the biting cold and her knees shook. She kicked off her rabbit-fur boots. The only part of her that wasn't bothered was her waist where she had tied Boris. She untied him and watched the only protection she had drop to the ground. She was determined to freeze.

"I'm going to stay like this all night," she whispered to the tree. It creaked and moaned as it bent low in the wind. "And when the sun comes up I'm going to take an ice cold shower and drip dry. I'll get pneumonia for sure. By tomorrow night, when everyone is sitting at the birthday dinner table, I'll be in the intensive care ward of the hospital. No one will blame me for the missing cake. Everyone will be sorry for all the mean things they ever did and all the worry they've caused me."

She could see her family bringing her home to die in her own bed, her own humble beginnings. "She was such a good child," her mother would say. "A saint," Grand would say. Lily would be so upset that she would stop seeing Claire altogether and she'd come back to their room. Everyone would mourn her for sixty years and they'd only wear blue because it was her favorite color and eat black food—black licorice, olives and watermelon seeds. A tear slipped down Maud's cheek as she wept for herself.

"I was so good and nobody noticed until it was too late," she cried. Suddenly, she heard a light knock on the door.

"Maudy, are you asleep?"

It was Grand. Maud practically leapt up into her bed. She pulled her covers over herself, her teeth still chattering from cold. The door slowly opened and Grand stepped inside.

"Tonight was our first performance," Grand said. "How'd it go?"

"We were a smash. Four curtain calls." Grand was just tall enough to lean against the top of the bed. Maud could see her colorful stage makeup in the dim light. She had gold sparkles on her eyelids. Maud gently touched one of her eyelids. Three gold sparkles came off on her fingertip.

"Are you all right, Maudy?" Maud nodded. "It's

freezing in here." Grand walked to the window and closed it. Maud inwardly thanked her for coming in to say goodnight when she did.

"Don't you want your rabbit fur boots?" Grand asked, picking them up from the floor and handing them to Maud before she had a chance to answer. As Maud slipped her feet into the soft warm boots she wondered if she should tell Grand about the cake.

"I can't wait for Lily's birthday dinner tomorrow," Grand said as she covered Maud with an extra blanket. "I thought I'd put on my oriental makeup and costume for the occasion. Doesn't that sound like fun?"

"Yes," Maud said half-heartedly. She felt like crying. She couldn't ruin Grand's fun by telling her about the cake. She'd have to fly this one solo. Maybe she'd run away and join the air force or something. Maud gazed longingly at Grand's back as she was about to go out the door.

"I'm a failure," she said softly.

"What?" Grand asked, walking back toward the bed. Maud wished Grand had been listening more carefully. It wasn't the sort of thing she wanted to repeat.

"I'm a failure."

"Nonsense. You're a great success," Grand said in a way that left no room for a single wisp of doubt. "Everyone does something well, Maudy, and it's foolish to deny it."

"For instance," Maud said.

"For instance, I know that I have an above average singing voice, I am a memorable character actor and I am an excellent companion." Grand had never been apologetic about her attributes, a fact which tended to shock some people who leaned toward modesty.

"What am I successful at?" Maud asked.

"What are you successful at?" Grand said as though she couldn't believe she was being asked. "At being my granddaughter, for one thing."

"That doesn't count."

"You're a success at a lot of things, Maudy."

"For instance," Maud said loudly. She wanted to know. She had to know.

"You're a good friend to John Henry, you're an imaginative cook, a fast runner and you make your old grandmother laugh."

Maud hated it when Grand called herself old.

"Is that enough for tonight?" Grand asked.

"I suppose." All of the things she had mentioned were true.

"I'll think up some more things at breakfast tomorrow. Goodnight, Maudy." She shut the door behind her.

Grand was right. She was good at a lot of things. She had always been an excellent sister (until she had eaten Lily's cake), she was a sound sleeper, a good eater and she had a terrific memory.

Tomorrow—Lily—Cake. Maud wished she wasn't so good at remembering. What would she do? She couldn't think of anything except making another one herself.

"That's it! I'll bake a cake!"

With her problem neatly resolved, she tied Boris around the bedpost for the night. She closed her eyes and visualized Lily's perfect chocolate cake with delicate yellow roses and pink script lettering on top. She opened her eyes and sighed. She knew that it would never work. She had made a cake only once before and it was two inches high with green icing. No one in the family, including herself, would eat it. She had ended up giving it to John Henry.

If only I had enough money to buy another cake, she thought. She looked across the room. She could barely see the outline of her mouse in the dark. No, thought Maud. She knew that if she used that money it would take her forever to replace it.

"I can't," Maud pleaded to the tree outside her window. "It's my flying lesson money. It's too important. I'm a flyer."

Suddenly, she heard steps coming toward her room again. Perhaps Grand was coming back with a new list of things she was successful at.

"Grand?" Maud asked as the door opened.

"No. It's me."

Lily appeared at Maud's bedside, her face red from the wind. The crisp smell of cold night air still clung to her clothes and skin hinting of some wonderful adventure that Maud would never know about.

"How are you feeling?"

"O.K." Maud could barely look at her she felt so guilty.

"What did you get me for my birthday? Emeralds or rubies?"

"Emeralds," Maud said.

"Good. I'll wear green tomorrow," Lily said and forced a little laugh. She walked out the door.

Maud sat up straight in bed and wondered if it was possible for an eleven year old to have a heart attack. She had been so worried about replacing Lily's cake that she had completely forgotten about getting her a birthday present.

She jumped out of bed, turned on the light and took her mouse down from the bureau. She spilled her fortune onto a pillow to prevent the coins from making a lot of noise, and counted. Eleven dollars and twenty-one cents. Dumping her loot back into the mouse, she secured the rubber stopper, turned off the light and got into bed again.

"I'm going to need that money for flying," Maud whispered. "I don't have enough to spare. Why should I spend it on Lily anyway? She's not so great."

Just then Maud noticed that her door had opened a crack.

"Maudy?" It was Lily again. "I thought I'd remind you that we're having a giant dinner tomorrow so don't stuff yourself at breakfast."

"Is Claire going to be there?" Maud asked sheepishly.

"No. This is a family birthday dinner. Besides, Claire couldn't come. Guess what?"

"What?"

"Grand got tickets for the whole family to see her in *The Mikado* tomorrow night."

"Will you sit next to me?"

"I guess so . . . You really miss me not being in here with you, don't you?"

Maud silently nodded as the door clicked shut. She closed her eyes and moaned softly. She would need a lot of rest before buying Lily's birthday cake tomorrow.

21

Countdown

"John Henry?"

"Uh-huh."

"How does your face feel?" Maud touched the bruised side of her nose as she waited for John Henry to answer.

"Bumpy. Mostly my nose sticks out."

"No, JH. How does your scar feel? Did your mother say you could go outside yet?"

"I went to the grocery store with her today and I get my stitches out next week."

"Good. Now listen carefully, JH. Are you listening carefully because I don't want to have to repeat this."

"O.K."

"I want you to meet me on the corner of Thirty-second and Second Avenue at exactly ten o'clock. Bring your wagon. Got that?"

"Uh-huh."

"Tell me what I just said."

"You said take my wagon to the corner."

"What corner?" Maud asked hysterically.

"The one with the newspapers and a mailbox."

"That's right and what time did I want you to

meet me?" There was a long silence. "Did you for-get, JH?"

"Yeah."

"At ten o'clock. Meet me at ten o'clock today. My life depends on it."

"Why?"

"I can't tell you."

"O.K. Bye."

"Wait," Maud screamed into the phone. "I haven't finished giving you your instructions. You have to load your wagon with dirty laundry."

"Why?"

"None of your business. Be at the corner of Thirty-second and Second Avenue at ten o'clock sharp with a wagon full of dirty laundry. Bye." She hung up before John Henry had a chance to irritate her any further.

Today, she had to replace Lily's birthday cake with another equally fantastic cake and it wasn't going to be easy. To accomplish her mission she knew that she must fly a straight course—wings level, nose up.

She quickly dressed and stood in the hall doing deep knee bends to clear her head. When the coast was clear Maud ran down to the basement to check the name of the bakery on the empty cake box. SHEILA'S SWEET SHOP was written on top of the large grease-stained box. She quickly wrote it down on a paper napkin and looked up the address in the tele-phone book, calculating its distance as only ten blocks from home.

That taken care of, she ate two Fig Newtons, a

handful of bird seed and half a glass of milk for quick energy. She ran back upstairs, found her watch and strapped it securely around her wrist. It was 9:50—ten minutes until take-off.

She removed her bank from its place of honor and opened it. She couldn't bear to look into its trusting mouselike face and furry little whiskers as she poured out its contents. Eleven dollars and twenty-one cents in quarters, nickels, dimes and pennies. Maud loved her money, especially when it was all together in one lovely lump.

Only three dollars and twelve cents fit into her wallet before it burst open. She put on her old blue sweater and filled each of its two pockets to the top. The weight of the coins stretched the loose-knit wool almost down to her knees. She put on her father's old air force flying jacket to cover the sagging sweater, grabbed her wallet and walked downstairs, careful not to jar any change out of her pockets. She decided to leave by the back door.

She was already in the kitchen when she noticed her mother standing in a corner pouring herself a cup of coffee.

"I thought you went out," she said, terrified her mother could see the coins bulging underneath the jacket.

"I did. I'm back. Miss me?" Maud nodded and smiled weakly. "Where did you get that old thing?" Mrs. Moser asked, pointing to the tattered leather flying jacket.

"Dad gave it to me," Maud said, pushing up one of the sleeves and glancing at her wristwatch. If she didn't leave now she would never make it to the meeting place in time.

"Do me a favor, Maudy. Will you get Lily's cake from the downstairs freezer for me? It has to have time to thaw out before dinner tonight."

Maud's life passed before her eyes in an instant. (She hadn't lived very long or it might have taken a few seconds more than an instant.)

"I'll do it later. I have to meet someone," Maud said quickly.

"Oh, forget it, Maudy," her mother said, walking toward the basement. "If you're busy, I'll do it."

Maud felt as though she were in a plane flying over a dangerous mountain range with a dense fog moving in. May Day. May Day. Visibility Zero. Check your bearings, she thought. Think clearly and check your bearings.

In a flash, Maud slid across the kitchen floor and flung herself against the basement door.

"What are you doing?" her mother gasped. "I thought you said you were too busy to get the cake now."

"It's not that," Maud cried, her mind still trying to fly its way out of the clouds. "It's just that if you bring a cake that big out of the freezer too soon it might get mushy."

"I suppose," Mrs. Moser said. "All right, Maudy. I'll leave it up to your discretion, but it has to be out of the freezer no later than eleven o'clock or it won't be ready in time."

"O.K., I promise," Maud said, peeling herself off the basement door. "You'll see, Mom. The cake will taste better this way, much better."

"Just don't forget," her mother said, walking away.

Eleven o'clock! Maud checked her watch. Exactly one hour and three minutes to complete her mission. She slammed the door behind her and ran down the street so fast eighteen cents fell out of one of her pockets.

22

Take-off

"What do you want me to write on it?" the woman asked, a tube of pink icing poised over the cake.

"HAPPY BIRTHDAY LILY," Maud said. "All in capital letters."

"That's funny," the woman said, squeezing out an L. "About two weeks ago a nice young girl came in here with her mother. I remember her because she was so fair, light skin, white-blonde hair. You know what I mean?"

Maud nodded. She wished that she had thought to go to the bathroom before leaving the house.

"I'm almost positive that she wanted me to write HAPPY BIRTHDAY LILY on her cake, too."

"Lily is a very popular name," Maud said, emptying the contents of her wallet on the counter.

"HAPPY BIRTHDAY DEBBIE, JUDY or KATHY are popular requests, but I've never been asked to write more than one HAPPY BIRTHDAY LILY in all the time I've worked here," said the woman, finishing the "Y" on "Lily." She dropped the cake in a box and closed the lid. "That will be nine dollars and seventeen cents."

"Will you break that down, please?" Maud asked. Grand often requested salesclerks to do that.

"Certainly," said the woman. "Nine dollars for the cake, including tax, seventeen cents for the personalized message. One cent for each letter."

Maud had taken off her oversized jacket and was shoveling handfuls of coins out of her sweater pockets. The bakery was becoming crowded with people. Maud pulled the last few coins out of her jeans pocket as fast as she could and put them on the counter.

It was sad parting with her money, the money she had lovingly doted over and cleaned with a felt rag every so often. Little by little it had grown with her over the months and now a stranger was counting it and throwing it roughly into her cash register with the rest of the neighborhood currency.

"You should have gone to the bank to get it changed into dollar bills," said an irritated woman who was standing in line behind her.

"I am a flier," Maud said, tired and cranky from the day's worries. "We never carry paper money. It blows away too easily."

"Everybody knows that," John Henry said, standing up straight, his hands on his holster, ready to shoot.

"And who are you?" the woman said with a sneer.

"I'm a cowboy," John Henry said. "We don't carry paper money either."

"Don't be such a copycat, JH. Now, help me with

this cake." They lowered the box into the wagon and covered it with dirty laundry.

"Helping your mom with the laundry today?" the bakery woman asked. Maud nodded and smiled sweetly.

"Here, take these cookies for the road," she said, handing her two chocolate chip cookies. "I like to see kids helping out their parents."

"Thanks." Maud led the way as John Henry pulled the heavy load behind them.

"Hey, don't forget your change," the bakery woman called after them. Maud motioned for John Henry to go collect it. Once they were on the crowded street Maud counted the remains of her dwindled fortune.

"One dollar and eighty-six cents," she sighed. "Boy, have I come down in the world."

"Cowboys don't need money," John Henry said. "They live off the land."

"Look around you, JH," Maud said, backing out of the way of a stream of people coming down the sidewalk. "How many cowboys do you see?" John Henry looked around and shrugged his shoulders.

"It's a jungle out here," Maud said, repeating something she sometimes heard her mother say. "Cowboys should stick to the wide open spaces and fliers should stay airborne." John Henry sighed and nodded.

"We're like worms out of dirt," he said, pulling the wagon behind him as he followed Maud down the street. She knew that he meant fish out of water, but she didn't say anything.

They had spent longer than she had planned in the bakery, but they still had eighteen minutes left before the eleven o'clock deadline. If she hurried she might have enough time to get Lily a present. They passed a record store and a clothes boutique, but Maud knew that records and clothes were too expensive. She was beginning to fear that she would be forced to show up empty-handed when they passed Riesler's Economy Drug Store. The window was plastered with signs advertising items on sale.

Two enormous eyes stared down at her from the window. Maud was momentarily startled until she realized that they were made of cardboard, part of a large sign advertising eyebrow pencils.

"Who would want to put that stuff on their eyebrows," John Henry said reading the sign with her.

"I don't know," Maud sighed. She stuck her hands deep into the flying jacket and walked past the drugstore. They would have to start back home soon.

"No one I know would do something as weird as that except maybe Claire." John Henry looked up at her questioningly. "She's this reject girl friend of Lily's. She wears red nail polish and . . ." Maud stopped suddenly.

"That's it! Eyebrow pencils. Lily will love them! Wait for me here," she ordered. She ran back to the drugstore before John Henry had a chance to protest.

Maud walked to the cosmetics area for assistance.

"Do you have any eyebrow pencils left?" she asked a woman standing behind a counter.

"What kind do you want?"

"The ones on sale," Maud said. The woman raised one neatly drawn eyebrow.

"We have several eyebrow items on sale. You'll have to be more specific."

"The magic ones in the sign on your window."

"Oh," she said and disappeared below the counter. She emerged holding two ordinary-looking pencils. "Parisian Magic, an excellent line. You're lucky. We happen to have two left. What is the complexion of the person you're buying these for?"

"Pale."

"I'm sorry, dear. We sold out of the light colors yesterday." She plucked the pencils out of Maud's hand.

"I want the darkest pencils you've got. I'm buying them for an actress," she said in her lowest and most serious voice. She didn't have any time to waste.

"I see," the woman said in a fog of confusion. "We have one black pencil and one brown. Which one would she prefer?"

"Both," Maud said. "One for each eye. Two for a dollar and fifty cents, right?"

The woman nodded and dropped them in a small bag as Maud pulled out the last of her riches.

While waiting to get her change she saw a jar of jerky sticks on a nearby shelf. She bought one with the few coins she had left.

It had started snowing while she was inside. Everything was covered with a light film of white. John Henry was sitting on the edge of the wagon with several dirty shirts piled in his lap. When Maud approached him she could see that he was shivering.

"Where were you?" he screamed.

"I'm sorry I took so long." She handed him the stick of dried beef. "Chew on this. It'll help you get warm faster. This is the stuff all the cowboys in the movies chew, JH. Beef jerky. Every cowboy keeps a supply of it with him on the trail. I think if you chew on it long enough it can even change the shape of your face . . . you know, make it look more ornery and cowboy-like."

John Henry ripped off the wrapper and began chewing wildly as Maud pulled the wagon the rest of the way home.

The mission was completed in time. The cake landed on the kitchen counter at precisely two minutes before eleven o'clock. Maud was not seen again until dinner that evening when she appeared in oriental costume and makeup with Grand. Her accomplice received a last minute invitation and appeared in cowboy attire, as usual.

"I thought this cake was supposed to be chocolate inside," Lily said as she sliced the first piece and passed it to Grand. Maud tried her best to look innocent while kicking John Henry under the table to make him stop looking so guilty.

"The salesclerk must have gotten them mixed up," Mrs. Moser said. "Oh, well, this looks delicious." Lily nodded.

As Maud smiled with relief, her face felt as though it were cracking from the heavy oriental makeup Grand had put on her.

"Grand, this makeup you put on my face makes me feel smothered," she said. Her eyes crossed as she tried looking down at her cheeks.

"Here," Grand said, slicing a piece of cake onto her fork and holding it in front of Maud. "Eat this. You'll feel better. It takes time to get used to wearing stage makeup. You won't even notice it once you've been acting for a while."

"But, Grand, I don't want to be an act—" Grand shoved the cake in her mouth before she had a chance to finish her protest.

"I have an announcement to make," Lily said, tapping the side of her water goblet with her spoon. She waited until all eyes were on her, sat up straight in her chair, paused dramatically and said, "I . . . have decided . . . to become a professional actress."

In the next minute, Mrs. Moser gasped, Mr. Moser clapped, John Henry burped and helped himself to another piece of cake and Grand jumped up and hugged Lily. When things finally settled down, Lily was beaming at everyone, clearly delighted that she was clever enough to be an actress and thirteen at the same time. Her right cheek had a big red mark where Grand had kissed her.

"Time for presents," Mrs. Moser said, placing an

armful of gifts on the dining room table. Lily tore into them with abandon. She got an oriental robe from Grand, a small wall mirror that her father had cut in the shape of a swan and a new skating sweater with her name embroidered on the front.

"What did you get me, John Henry?" Lily asked teasingly. John Henry's face flushed deep claret red and he looked at Maud for help.

"Can't help you this time, JH," she said. John Henry pulled a half-chewed piece of beef jerky from his holster and extended it toward Lily.

"I think I'll take a raincheck," she said.

Maud reached down for the bag next to her chair and placed it on the table in front of Lily. "To you from me," she said, hovering over her sister to get a close-up of her reaction when she saw what was inside.

"Emeralds?" Lily asked, grinning. Maud shook her head.

"Better than emeralds." Lily stuck her hand in the bag and pulled out the two pencils. Her face registered disappointment.

"Pencils," she said rolling them over in her hands. "Thanks, Maud, but couldn't you at least have gotten the kind with erasers on the end?"

"Look at the label!" Maud shouted. "Those aren't regular pencils. Those are Parisian Magic eyebrow pencils. Now you can have dramatic eyes," she said, quoting the advertisement. She leaned over and whispered in Lily's ear, "You won't have to leave home, now."

Lily jumped up from her chair. "You're a genius, Maudy. Why didn't I think of eyebrow pencils?" Maud shrugged her shoulders and smiled sheepishly. "I'm going to try them right now. Grand, will you give me a lesson in theatrical makeup?" Without a word, Grand scooped up Lily's eyebrow pencils, took Lily by the arm and they disappeared toward the upstairs bathroom.

"Well, I guess that's that until next year," Mrs. Moser said, getting up to clear the dishes. As she walked past Maud into the kitchen, Maud noticed that her mother smelled like a field of roses instead of a pine forest. She must have gotten some new bath salts. Everyone changes, thought Maud. Even my own mother. But I'll never change. I'll always want to be a flier.

I'm eating my flying lessons, Maud thought sadly as she started on her third piece of cake.

"How old do you have to be to fly, Dad?" she asked.

"Sixteen."

Five more years to save up for flying lessons, she thought. I ought to have an army of mice filled with money by then.

Maud was sitting in her room on a Sunday afternoon when she heard the doorbell ring. She jumped down the stairs, two at a time and raced to the door.

"Hi. Where's Lily?" Claire asked, pushing the door and Maud aside as she invited herself in. Before she had a chance to answer, Lily was at Claire's side. Lily's dark eyebrows danced up and down on her forehead as she whispered secrets to Claire and they walked off to her room together. Maud heard the familiar click of Lily's door locking.

She went back upstairs without thinking once about sitting outside her sister's door. She didn't have time. She was meeting a new friend from school at the skating rink. She didn't care anymore how ridiculous she looked on the skating rink. Sarah looked just as bad. They both had weak ankles. Sarah said weak ankles were a sign of high intelligence.

On her way to the kitchen she glanced in the hall mirror. Her hair was back to mud brown again. What a relief. She stuffed some Fig Newtons into her skates alongside her ankle supports. She and Sarah would eat them later. She added two extra in case John Henry showed up with his brothers.

Maud slammed the door on her way out. She took three deep breaths to clear her head. She would take the shortcut to the rink that Sarah had shown her.

It was a clear sky, a few scattered clouds in the distance, mild winds, good visibility—it would be a terrific day for flying.